He Had Only Two Days Left With Her.

Zayad's gut clenched. He was a fool, but he did not want her to know who he was. For the first time in his life, someone was not aware of his role, his fortune, his title. Mariah cared for him as a man, not a prince. And for that, he would always be in her debt. Starting with her court case.

"Dinnertime."

He turned, and his body went rock hard, fast. There she stood, moonlight at her back, draped in a thin white cotton tank and little white cotton shorts. She looked ready for bed, not for dinner.

But then again, he mused as he walked to her, he could always be persuaded to eat dessert first.

Dear Reader,

Thank you for choosing Silhouette Desire, where this month we have six fabulous novels for you to enjoy. We start things off with *Estate Affair* by Sara Orwig, the latest installment of the continuing DYNASTIES: THE ASHTONS series. In this upstairs/downstairs-themed story, the Ashtons' maid falls for an Ashton son and all sorts of scandal follows. And in Maureen Child's *Whatever Reilly Wants…*, the second title in the THREE-WAY WAGER series, a sexy marine gets an unexpected surprise when he falls for his suddenly transformed gal pal.

Susan Crosby concludes her BEHIND CLOSED DOORS series with *Secrets of Paternity*. The secret baby in this book just happens to be eighteen years old…. Hmm, there's quite the story behind that revelation. The wonderful Emilie Rose presents *Scandalous Passion*, a sultry tale of a woman desperate to get back some steamy photos from her past lover. Of course, he has a price for returning those pictures, but it's not money he's after. *The Sultan's Bed*, by Laura Wright, continues the tales of her sheikh heroes with an enigmatic male who is searching for his missing sister and finds a startling attraction to her lovely neighbor. And finally, what was supposed to be just an elevator ride turns into a very passionate encounter, in *Blame It on the Blackout* by Heidi Betts.

Sit back and enjoy all of the smart, sensual stories Silhouette Desire has to offer.

Happy reading,

Melissa Jeglinski

Melissa Jeglinski
Senior Editor
Silhouette Desire

Please address questions and book requests to:
Silhouette Reader Service
U.S.: 3010 Walden Ave., P.O. Box 1325, Buffalo, NY 14269
Canadian: P.O. Box 609, Fort Erie, Ont. L2A 5X3

THE SULTAN'S BED

LAURA WRIGHT

Silhouette®

Desire

Published by Silhouette Books
America's Publisher of Contemporary Romance

SILHOUETTE BOOKS

ISBN 0-373-76661-0

THE SULTAN'S BED

Copyright © 2005 by Laura Wright

This edition published by arrangement with Harlequin Books S.A.

Visit Silhouette Books at www.eHarlequin.com

Printed in U.S.A.

Books by Laura Wright

Silhouette Desire

Cinderella & the Playboy #1451
Hearts Are Wild #1469
Baby & the Beast #1482
Charming the Prince #1492
Sleeping with Beauty #1510
Ruling Passions #1536
Locked Up with a Lawman #1553
Redwolf's Woman #1582
A Bed of Sand #1607
The Sultan's Bed #1661

LAURA WRIGHT

has spent most of her life immersed in the world of acting, singing and competitive ballroom dancing. But when she started writing romance, she knew she'd found the true desire of her heart! Although born and raised in Minneapolis, Laura has also lived in New York City, Milwaukee and Columbus, Ohio. Currently she is happy to have set down her bags and made Los Angeles her home. And a blissful home it is—one that she shares with her theatrical production manager husband, Daniel, and three spoiled dogs. During those few hours of downtime from her beloved writing, Laura enjoys going to art galleries and movies, cooking for her hubby, walking in the woods, lazing around lakes, puttering in the kitchen and frolicking with her animals. Laura would love to hear from you. You can write to her at P.O. Box 5811, Sherman Oaks, CA 91413 or e-mail her at laurawright@laurawright.com.

To a wonderful friend, amazing writer, brilliant critique partner—and all around fabulous woman: Jennifer Apodaca.

Prologue

"**O**ur father sired another child."

With those words Zayad Al-Nayhal, Sultan of Emand, executed a perfect rotation and plunged his sword into his imaginary target's chest. When he pulled back, he fought to keep his footing on the smooth stones of the large terrace that spanned the entire third floor of his palace. His arms were tight, his body exhausted and he could plainly see that his right hand bled.

It was no wonder after three and one-half hours of exercise.

Correction—of diversion.

Last night he had received a letter from his father's aide, a man who had passed away quietly just one week ago. The letter had been delivered by the aide's son and had contained a confession of such emotional intensity,

Zayad immediately had called his brother and asked him to come home. Knowing nothing but the agitation in his brother's voice, Sakir had agreed and been en route within the hour.

Through the night, Zayad had attempted to sleep. But that had been a fool's endeavor. At two-thirty in the morning he had escaped his empty bed and his cold silk sheets and made his way to the terrace, prepared to wield his sword, to sweat and to await his brother.

Zayad returned to the present, heard the palace bustle with activity on the floors below, and nodded at the four servants who stood in readiness at opposite ends of the terrace. Beyond the palace walls the sun was slowly creeping its way across the desert, eager to plant itself firmly on the horizon.

It was daybreak, and his brother was finally here.

Swathed in a backdrop of stone balconies, terracotta silk curtains and golden domes that stretched high into the blue sky, Sakir Al-Nayhal stood tall, his arms crossed at his chest, a frown tugging at his full mouth. "You have done many things to get me back to Emand, but creating this story—"

His sword at his side, Zayad shook his head. "This is no story, brother."

"I do not believe you," Sakir returned. "I have left a beautiful pregnant wife because you sounded as though—"

"As though there were an emergency?" Zayad lifted his eyebrow.

"Yes. And I find you here trifling with your sword."

His eyes fixed on his brother, Zayad steered the tip of his blade toward a small round table situated beside a man-made waterfall and a hundred flowering plants. On the table was a gold tray containing Zayad's uneaten breakfast. And beside the plate sat a two-page letter, its thin edges flickering in the warm breeze. "Draka wrote that letter to me before he died. What he has to say is quite extraordinary and of such import that I thought it wise to take you from Rita."

Sakir stared at the letter but made no move to pick it up. "What does it say?"

"It states that twenty-six years ago our father traveled to America to meet with the two senators of California on modern oil-drilling practices." His lips thinned with irritation. "There he met a woman."

Sakir's brows knit together. "A woman?"

"She was a young aide who worked for one of the senators. It seems that our father was instantly captivated by her beauty and spirit. He asked her to take a meal with him that night, and she accepted. After dinner they took a long drive up the coast—" he paused, inhaled deeply "—then she invited him to her home."

It was a moment before Sakir spoke, but his eyes glittered with bewilderment. "This is very hard for me to believe. Our father detested Americans."

"I thought so, as well, but Draka says that the sultan told him that this woman was different."

For the second time in twenty-four hours, anger inched its way into Zayad's blood, and he hated himself for it. He was no romantic. He did not believe in true love, at least for himself. He understood the ways of men in his position—even married men. But his father had been different. Or so Zayad had thought. The Sultan had never taken another woman to his bed. Only his wife. He had always claimed his love for Zayad's mother was true and without competition and that the old ways had not, and would not, claim him.

"How long was our father in America?" Sakir asked.

"Three days."

"And his nights were spent with this woman?"

"It would appear so."

"You spoke of a child," Sakir said, his jaw tight.

"One month after the sultan returned to Emand, the woman contacted Draka."

"And?" Sakir prompted when Zayad paused.

"She claimed she was with child. She claimed the sultan was her child's father. She wished to speak with him, to tell him of this news."

"And what did our father say to her?"

Zayad walked to the balcony, searched for calm in the rugged landscape, the desert floor and the mountains beyond. "Draka did not tell our father of her call or her news."

"What?" Sakir fairly snapped.

"Draka did not believe that the woman was speaking the truth."

"Yes, but an investigation should have been made."

"Of course it should have." Zayad's gaze fell to the acres of lush garden that held fruit trees and herbs, but more importantly, held the grave of his youngest brother, Hassan. The boy had died many years ago in a military training accident, and for Zayad, grief still spread through his bones every time he thought about losing his brother.

Butterflies flew and fed at the red and purple flowers by Hassan's grave-site. A reminder that his spirit remained, yet would always be able to fly free. Zayad knew in that moment that even if there was the smallest possibility that he and Sakir had another sibling, he had to pursue it.

"What are you thinking, brother?" Sakir asked.

Zayad turned, his back to his beloved land. "This is a personal matter, a family matter, but one that needs to be addressed. I am thinking that at long last an investigation will be made."

Sakir nodded. "Yes. We will find this child."

"*I* will find the child."

"But—"

"As you said, brother, you have a beautiful pregnant wife at home who needs you. You cannot be away from her for longer than a few days. I feel selfish in taking you away for that long, but I was convinced a phone call would not do here."

"You were right."

"And I am right about you going home and staying there with your Rita."

Sakir's mouth formed a grim line, but he nodded. "The child's DNA must be tested."

"It will be. But, Sakir, you understand that this is no child. Not anymore."

"Of course. He must be a full-grown man by now."

With a quick flick of his wrist Zayad stabbed at the letter with the tip of his sword, piercing the paper. He thrust it at his brother. "Read the last paragraph."

Sakir slipped the paper from the blade and read.

With curious eyes Zayad watched his brother, watched as his face turned from interest to unease to shock.

When Sakir finally looked up, his green eyes were wide. "A girl?"

"Yes." Zayad had been just as stunned when he had read this. After three men of Al-Nayhal, the thought of a girl child born to his father hadn't occurred to Zayad.

"Where is she?" Sakir asked.

Walking over to the table, Zayad grasped the glass of plum juice from his tray and drained it. "She lives in a town one hour from Los Angeles, California. It is called Ventura."

"When do you leave?"

"Tomorrow morning. My investigation is already under way. I must have more information on this woman and her life before I leave, before I attempt to get close to her. I will fly with you to the States, then continue on to California."

"Then what?"

"I will live as an American, get to know this Jane Hefner, see if she is truly an Al-Nayhal, see if she is capable of knowing and accepting her truth."

"You will keep me updated, yes?"

"Of course." Zayad motioned for a servant to come and remove his breakfast tray and for another to take his sword. They were swift in their tasks, and soon Zayad and Sakir were heading inside the palace.

Sakir stopped at the doorway to the ballroom, turned to Zayad and grinned. "We could have a sister."

Not sharing his brother's enthusiasm, Zayad continued walking down the marble hallway. "Do not get your hopes up just yet, Sakir. We could have a sister. But we also could have an impostor."

One

Are all men jerks, or what?

Mariah Kennedy stepped out of her '92 Escort—sans air-conditioning—and into the ninety-degree California weather.

Gorgeous, brilliant, charming—ten million dollars to his name—and yet he refuses to pay child support for his three-year-old twins.

She slammed the car door shut.

Sweat beaded at the base of her tight blond bun and threatened to drop down the back of her faux Chanel suit as she stalked up the stone pathway to her ancient—though still very charming—duplex. The early summer wind whipped off the ocean's surface just a half a mile away, trying to cool her skin as well as her I'm-so-going-to-lose-this-case mood.

No. All men can't be jerks. Dad was a real stand-up guy. It must be all the gorgeous, overly successful and far too irresistible ones that earn that label.

Mariah reached the front door and, in her usual style, fumbled around in her purse for her keys while simultaneously bending down to snatch up the newspaper she never had time to read until she returned home from work at five.

Normally she accomplished both tasks without a problem.

But today was all about problems.

The headline, Sun Exposure Blamed For Weight Gain, screamed up at her, and she hesitated a second too long in picking it up.

Something rustled behind her. Without a thought she straightened and whirled around—all at the same time.

Not a good combo.

In that same inept, awkward and very humiliating style that had plagued her all morning in the judge's chambers, she ran smack-dab into a heavily muscled chest.

A strange cross between a hiccup and a gasp erupted from her throat, and she dropped her purse. The contents spilled out all over the walkway, except for a red pen and an extra pair of nylons, which sailed west into the hydrangea bushes.

"Dammit!" Mariah dropped to her knees.

In seconds the man was beside her.

"Don't worry about it," she said, shoving lipstick and iron pills into her purse as quickly as she could. "I've got everything under control here."

"All signs would point to the contrary."

Mariah stopped her manic sidewalk cleanup for a moment. In the seconds before, when she'd been off balance, smashing headfirst into strangers and letting her purse travel south, she'd barely glimpsed the man beside her.

Dark…tall—that's about it.

She glanced up.

Heat, and not from the sun this time, oozed into her bones. Never in her life had she seen the cover of *GQ* magazine live and in person. Yet here he was. Dark, soulful eyes that assessed her; short, well-groomed black hair; sharp, angular features that screamed exquisite breeding; and a full mouth that she was sure had driven far too many sane females mad with desire.

He was the kind of man who could easily utter in your ear as he was nibbling on your neck, "I'm female poison. Beware."

She forced her pulse to slow, but it did little good as the man sat back on his haunches and gave her an amused look.

He was probably midthirties, she guessed, and ridiculously handsome. He had that look of supreme confidence in his manner and expression, the kind that usually made such a stellar impression in court—both on the men and the women. Though this man was not dressed in lawyerly garb. No suit and tie. No, he wore a simple black T-shirt under an exquisitely tailored white shirt. Of course, on that lean, hard body they looked anything but simple.

Mariah hated herself for feeling weak-kneed and ultra feminine. And she wanted to laugh. This impossibly beautiful man was no doubt the new tenant Mrs. Gill had told her about yesterday.

The tenant Mrs. Gill had referred to as "a sweet young man."

The "sweet, young man" raised an eyebrow at her. "I did not mean to insult you. It is just that you seem quite out of sorts."

A husky baritone accompanied by a sexy accent. She mentally rolled her eyes. *Perfect.* "I'm not out of sorts at all."

He picked up her ratty copy of *Women Who Love Men Are Morons,* glanced at it for a moment, then held it out to her. "If I could offer a suggestion…"

She snatched up the book. "What? That maybe next time I should look where I'm going?"

"There is this, yes." He stood, offered her a hand. "Slowing one's pace is also good."

She took his hand, let him pull her to her feet. "I've never been any good at slow."

He didn't acknowledge her comment but continued with his advice. "And I also find that apologizing for situations you have caused is a very admirable trait."

At that she gave him a half smile. Maybe she was wrong about all gorgeous, smart and charming men being jerks. "It *is* admirable, and I appreciate the apology. You did scare the heck out of—"

"No. I was speaking of you."

Maybe not.

"Excuse me?" she said.

"It was you who ran into me, was it not?"

"Yes, but it was an accident."

"I do not believe in accidents. But even so, an apology is in order."

Everything in her lawyerly bones urged her to argue the subject, but after a day like today—when every question, every word had been challenged—she just wasn't up for it.

Yet she wasn't in the mood to apologize, either.

So she went halfsies.

"I feel deep regret for plowing into you." She brightened. "How's that?"

He didn't look appeased. "I suppose it will have to do, Miss…" His dark gaze traveled over her.

"Mariah Kennedy," she said, through a severe case of the belly flips.

"I am Zayad Fandal. I live beside you."

Of course he did. Her guess had been right on target. After all, it was her destiny to live beside, work beside, be divorced from and argue against tall, dark and irritatingly gorgeous men.

Remember…look but don't touch, M.

"Nice to meet you, Mr. Fandal. Welcome to the neighborhood. And again, deep regret about the head in the chest thing." She turned to her door and shoved the key in the lock.

"Wait a moment, Miss Kennedy."

She glanced over her shoulder just in time to catch him checking out her backside. "Yes?"

"I wonder if I might ask you something?"

She mentally shook her head. *Not interested, playboy. But thanks.* After the hellish divorce that had claimed her life for nearly four years, then seeing the daily nightmares that her female clients went through with guys just like this one, she had sworn to only date men under five-seven with unhypnotic eyes and thin lips. Men who neither dazzled her brain nor her body.

Stupid idea? Yes, probably. But safe. Very, very safe. And she was all about safety now.

"What is it, Mr. Fandal?" she asked with a patient smile.

"I wish to know if your roommate, Jane Hefner, is at home."

What a loser!

Waves of embarrassment moved over Mariah as she took in the tender look in this guy's eyes. Here she was thinking Mr. Next Door was coming on to her when he was clearly interested in Jane. And who could blame him? Her beautiful, raven-haired roommate had men drooling night and day. Mariah's dirty-blond hair and short, curvy figure were no match for Jane's slender, long legs and bright green eyes. No doubt Zayad had met Jane this morning—without the sweat, the acerbic lawyerspeak and the head-on collision—and wanted to ask her out.

What a total idiot.

"Jane's working right now, but she'll be back later."

"Thank you." He grinned. "Goodbye, Miss Kennedy."

He inclined his head, then walked past her down the steps before disappearing into a shiny black SUV. Her hand on the doorknob, Mariah stared after him thinking about how great he looked, both from the front and from the back.

Mariah released a weighty breath. More than anything in the world she'd love to delve into a nice sum-

mer romance. She had been pretty lonely lately. No
dates, even with the under-five-seven crowd. A summer
fling with Mr. Tall, Dark and Handsome could be fun.
But fantasies needed to remain just that. Men like that
one cheated and lied and jumped ship when the going
got rough.

For a moment Mariah just stood there mulling over
her thoughts, her beliefs and theories. It wasn't a pretty
picture. If truth be told, she hated how bitter she'd become. Sure, it had made her a better lawyer, but what
had it done to her as a woman?

She couldn't help but remember a time, long ago and
oh-so far away, when she'd lived in an eternal spring-
time. Love had bitten her and sent her reeling. Like
some Disney cartoon. But a man had stripped her raw
of that feeling and taken her trust and hope along with
it.

Her faux leather briefcase felt like a bag of rocks as
she headed into the house to her beloved Little Debbie
snack cakes and later a long, hot bath.

The sultan had taken a risk in coming to America
with only a handful of security. But he refused to be
under guard. He had brought just three men, and all
were under strict orders to protect only when commanded.

With a quick glance in the rearview mirror at the
beautiful and highly spirited woman who lived next
door, Zayad pulled away from the curb and headed
down the street. Behind him another car also moved
from the curb. Zayad had an almost irresistible urge to
floor the black Escalade and give his men something

to chase, but as always, he would resist impulses and desires that did not serve his country's purposes.

His cell phone rang. He took his time in answering. "Yes, Harin?"

"Where are you going, sir?"

"To the beach." His body was tight. He needed exercise, something to calm his nerves. His sword lay in the backseat, ready for work.

"If I may suggest Dove Cove, sir. It is deserted at this time. You will not be disturbed."

"Very good, but I will go alone."

"Sir—"

"Take the next exit and return home. I will let you know when I have need of you again." Zayad snapped the phone shut. He was only going to the beach. Surely he could protect himself if the need arose. He was, after all, a master swordsman. A man who had studied under the great warrior, Ohanda. All knew that at the age of twelve the young sultan had been able to hear a predator—animal or otherwise—ten feet away and easily take him down.

But as an adult Zayad also understood that in certain situations it was wise to have protection. His people must have him back safe and sound. As must his son, who was young yet, just thirteen, and not ready to take his father's place as ruler if something were to happen.

The thought of his son sent Zayad's mind racing toward another child. A female. One who could be his father's daughter. A young girl who might never have known she was of royal blood. A girl who might never have known she had two brothers who would give much to know her.

Zayad glanced to the seat beside him and flipped open a file folder. A photograph stared up at him. A beautiful young woman with the late sultan's cheekbones and Sakir's green eyes. Zayad did not need a DNA test. This woman felt like family even in her photograph. But he knew it would be necessary for others. So, while his doctor performed the test, he would get to know her. Tonight.

A child's excitement moved through him. He had been born to rule. To remain impassive. He had been taught to live well, think great thoughts and be lenient when the time arose and severe when it was demanded. And like his brother, Sakir, understand that wishes and dreams were for others and death came too quickly with little mercy. But then there was the rare occasion, like the birth of his son, when the purest of joy had threatened to overtake him. Meeting his sister for the first time certainly would be one of those moments. He would allow himself the pang of excitement.

Zayad swung left at the farm stand and headed toward Dove Cove. He would only take a few hours of exercise on the warm sand, as he needed to return to the duplex. He had much to accomplish, including keeping his true mission a secret to those around him. His council, like the men he had brought with him—save Fandal—believed his purpose here to be one of rest and relaxation. Of course, they did not question his living quarters or his interest in his neighbor. They dared not. And Zayad expected that they would remain devoted servants for his two-week stay.

Ah, yes, he thought. Two weeks with no questions, no interruptions and no diversions.

A pretty blond attorney with a voluptuous body and angry eyes the color of the hot Emand sand at sunset flashed into his mind. His sister's roommate was tough and spirited, and if he had more time, he might consider pursuing an affair with her.

His hands tightened on the steering wheel.

His father had once said, "A man is not a man without restraint. Especially in matters of the state."

Sea air blew in through his window, but Zayad did not calm in its caress. The irony was too plain. His father, the great sultan, had overlooked his own counsel when coming to America.

Should he expect any less from his son?

Two

Jane Hefner was to food what Manolo Blahnik was to shoes.

Perfection.

Mariah took another bite of the sublimely delicious, strangely refreshing basil ice cream and sighed. "Tell me again why you have to leave?"

Jane folded a pale yellow shirt with faultless precision and gently placed it between two pieces of parchment in her suitcase. "The restaurant wants publicity, so it's me to the rescue. And teaching some pampered movie star how to make veal piccata and garlic mashed potatoes for her next film might sound like a chore to some people, but to me it's—"

"A dream come true?"

Jane laughed. "Hey, it's Cameron Reynolds."

"Right." Mariah sat on the bed, folded a pair of jeans for Jane. "You understand that you're forcing me to eat a week's worth of frozen dinners?"

Jane eased the jeans from Mariah and refolded them. "Dry fish sticks, watery mashed potatoes, mushy pea-and-carrot medley and fig compote?" She shrugged. "I don't see the problem."

"You may be a genius in the kitchen, but you have absolutely no compassion on my poor stomach."

"I know. But I'll be back before you know it."

Mariah paused, realized how pathetic she sounded with all the Miss Lonely Hearts prattle. Seemed she relied on her friend too much. After her divorce from Alan, she'd clung to Jane as a sister, as a friend—the way she had when they were kids, when her parents had died and her feeble grandmother had given her a home but little else.

Mariah fell back on the bed. "Can I just say that your boss is pretty ballsy for making you go on such short notice?"

"It's cash, M."

Jane's sudden serious tone and slight grimace made Mariah pause, ease up on the semiphony guilt trip. She knew Jane was saving up to open her own restaurant. It was her dream. And as her friend, Mariah wasn't about to be anything but all-the-way supportive. "All right, but if your boss doesn't compensate you big time for this, you know I can always sue him. Or, hey, I have a friend down at the board of health and he's really into closing down Italian restaurants." Mariah leaned on her elbows. "I think his brother was taken out by the mob or something."

Jane laughed, shut her suitcase. "Thanks, M. I'll think about it."

"No you won't. You're too damn nice to think about it."

She grinned. "So, I hear our new neighbor's moved in. Have you met him yet?"

Mariah rolled her eyes. "Have I met him? You could say that."

"What happened?"

"Let's just say I was in rare form—there were bruises and razor-sharp banter on the menu."

Jane laughed, sat down beside her. "Is he good-looking, or a toad like the last one?"

"Why are you asking me all this? You've met him, too."

"No, I haven't."

"Sure you have."

Jane shook her head.

Mariah blinked at her. "Maybe you said hi in passing or something, because he knows you."

"He knows me? What are you talking about?"

"He asked about you when he bumped into me—well, when I bumped into him. He wanted to know when you'd be home. It was like you'd met and talked and he was more than ready to ask you out."

Jane sniffed. "That's bizarre. Maybe Mrs. Gill told him about us, and after he met you he wanted to meet me…some neighborly, friendly kind of thing?"

"I dunno." Mariah shrugged. "But whatever his story is, be careful. He's trouble."

"Why?" Jane slid her feet into a pair of pink flip-flops that were placed neatly by the foot of the bed. "Because he's tall, dark and handsome?"

"For a start."

All humor dropped away from Jane's pretty face. She put a hand on Mariah's shoulder and took a breath. "Listen, M, someday you're going to have to see the world and every man in it with fresh eyes."

Mariah bristled, looked away. "I don't know what you mean."

"Yes, you do."

"Yeah, all right, I do. But that day's not today."

"Okay." Jane gave her a huge hug and said, "I'll call you," then stood, grabbed her suitcase and left the room.

After she had gone, Mariah headed into the kitchen to make herself one of the aforementioned TV dinners and contemplate her next move in the custody case she was working on. Her client's ex was smart and had hidden his affairs well. It was going to take some serious digging to find anything she could use.

When the breaded fish and compote were ready, she went outside and sat at the pretty picnic bench Jane had set up on the brick patio. The backyard looked lovely bathed in the night's light. Moon, stars, a few clouds...and soggy carrot-and-pea medley.

Ah, did it get any better than this?

"May I join you?"

Mariah gave a tiny jump, then glanced over her shoulder. Her new neighbor was walking through his patio doors toward her. He looked unbelievably handsome in the moonlight, with that dark-eyes-dark-hair-dark-tailored-clothes thing happening. He was also clean shaven, and it made all the sharp angles in his face look harder and sexier.

Her heart kicked to life in her chest, but she held fast

to a calm exterior. "I have some square fish and a few peas left, if you're interested."

His mouth curved into a smile as he sat opposite her at the picnic table. "I am not very hungry, but thank you."

"Just checking out the backyard? Or were you looking for someone?"

"Perhaps a little of both."

"Jane's not here."

His gaze went thoughtful. "I did not say I was looking for Jane."

"You didn't have to." Her tone sounded dry and acerbic, but he didn't seem to notice.

He said, "Perhaps I was looking for you."

Her heart literally fluttered. Foolish, foolish girl. "And why would that be?"

"Perhaps I wish to know more about this—" he studied her with a lazy, hooded gaze "—fiery woman who lives beside me."

Fiery! She nearly blushed.

Nearly.

"Well, there's not much to tell," she said, running her fork back and forth through the fig compote.

"I doubt that."

Lord, he had extraordinary eyes—so black, but flecked with gold. A woman could get lost in those eyes if she wasn't careful. Good thing Mariah was careful.

"Listen," she said with more regret in her tone than she would have liked. "I've got a ton of work to get to, so I'll say good—"

"What kind of work do you do?"

"I'm a lawyer."

His brow lifted a fraction.

"I help women who've been treated badly in their marriages get what they deserve."

"Interesting. And what do they deserve?"

"It depends. But first and foremost, respect. If they've given up their careers to take care of the home, I help them gain financial stability. If they've been cheated on during their marriage, their self-esteem robbed from them, I help them find a new life. Which is just like the case I'm working on now—"

Mariah came to a screeching halt. What was she doing? This man was no friend, no confidant, and here she was about to tell him the ins and outs of her case.

"What were you about to say, Miss Kennedy?"

She stood and grabbed the remains of her dinner. "Nothing, just that I'm working on a case and I'd better get inside and get to it."

She started to walk away, but he stopped her. "Miss Kennedy?"

She turned. "Yes?"

"You do not like men, do you?"

Walls shot up around her like steel plates. "Excuse me?"

He shrugged nonchalantly. "You make them sound like the enemy."

She lifted her chin. "In court, they are." And in life, her life, she thought, they weren't terribly far from that. She gave him a little wave. "Good night, Mr. Fandal," she said and headed into the house, where she could think and breathe again.

Moments later she had rid herself of "dinner" and

was walking into the bathroom. What she needed was a long, hot bath, to get that man's questions, comments and deliciously probing gaze out of her mind.

Hate men! What a notion.

Sure, she didn't trust men, she thought as she turned on the hot-water tap and let the tub fill up. There was a big difference.

Peeling off her clothes, she spotted her reflection in the mirror and took a moment to look herself over. The view surprised her a little. Under those bargain power suits of hers lay a pretty nice figure.

Her hands found their way to her flat stomach, up her rib cage to her large breasts. Her skin was pale and so sensitive, and as she ran her fingers over her nipples, she wanted to cry. She hadn't been touched in four years, and even then it had been seldom, as Alan had been far too busy making his mistress happy to help his wife find some pleasure.

She bit her lip. The truth was, she didn't hate men at all. In fact, if the right one came along, she was ready to go crazy with desire. But the fear in her heart was stronger than her need, and she couldn't imagine that changing anytime soon.

She turned away from the mirror and stepped into the hot bath.

Zayad cursed and pitched the bag of microwave popcorn across the room. The corn was black as night and had thoroughly stunk up the two-bedroom duplex he would be calling home for the next two weeks.

"I could hire a staff, Your Royal Highness."

Zayad turned, his back to the kitchen counter, and

eyed his aide and the closest thing he had to a friend—
the man from whom he had borrowed his last name.
"No, Fandal. I have told you there can be no show of
wealth and consequence. And do not call me 'Your
Highness.'"

"Yes, Your—" Fandal lifted his chin. "Yes, sir."

Zayad turned around, opened the cupboards, found
nothing as simple as the popcorn was purported to be
and moved on to the refrigerator. "I was hoping to
bring something with me when I meet with my sister this evening. An offering, a meal. But alas, I am
without."

"Flowers are usually well received, sir."

"I am to meet my sister, Fandal, not court the lovely
Miss Kennedy."

"Of course, sir." With a quick bow of understanding,
Fandal went to the bag of ruined popcorn and began to
clean up the mess.

Court the lovely Miss Kennedy? Zayad sniffed. His
mouth was without restraint. Perhaps because he could
not get the woman out of his head after their little dis-
cussion in the yard. It was most irritating. She had looked
so soft, so appealing, as she verbally annihilated her
client's ex-husband.

"May I say that the golden-haired woman seems unlike the women in our country," Fandal remarked with
just a hint of warning in his tone.

"She is at that." Blond, fair, a lioness with claws
outstretched. But something warned him that once
tamed, once her anger was released and desire ruled her
body, Mariah Kennedy would not let go those claws.
"Not that I would pursue it, but I imagine an affair

would not be casual with her. I fear that most American women want far more than a lover."

"Is it not true for all women, sir?"

"Not the women of my acquaintance."

"There was one."

The words had slipped from Fandal's lips far too easily. Zayad stopped short, his blood thundering in his ears at the memory of the woman who had left his company and that of her son with little regret. Turning around, he stood over a sheepish Fandal. "As you know, Meyaan did not want a true marriage. She did not want to share my life—or her son's, for that matter. She wanted to benefit from my power and the comfort allowed by the riches of a sultan." His chin lifted, though his ire sank deeper into his belly. "And she received both. But in the end I was the victor. I received the far more precious gift."

His face still ashen from his foolish remark, Fandal had the good sense to turn the subject to Zayad's child. "And how is His Highness?"

"Redet is well, happy at school." Getting far too mature at thirteen. Zayad missed his little boy.

Just then a loud thud reverberated off the walls. Zayad and Fandal ceased talking. Glancing around, they listened for a clue to its origin. When none came, Zayad uttered, "What the hell was that?"

Fandal shook his head. "I know not."

A woman's cry came next.

"Stay here," Zayad commanded. "I will go."

"Your Royal Highness, it could be dangerous."

"It is from next door. It could be my sister."

"I will go with you."

But Zayad was already at the door. "Do not leave this

house, Fandal, or you will find yourself swimming back to Emand. Are we clear?"

"Yes, sir."

"And say nothing to the others." Zayad was out of his house and at Jane and Mariah's door within seconds. He knocked swiftly, but there was no response. He gripped the door handle, but it was locked.

His chest constricted and he did not think, only reacted. He stepped back and lunged at the door with all of his strength. The lock pitched but remained intact. He tried again. Then again. Finally the lock collapsed and he was inside.

Three

"...I know I should have photographs of him with that other woman, but I can't find a thing, Miss Kennedy. Please call me back, okay?"

Through the pain in her wrist and ankle, Mariah listened to the end of her client's message, then the beep of her answering machine.

Nude, angry and lying in quasifetal position on the bathroom floor, Mariah sincerely wished she'd installed a telephone next to the bathtub. Such luxury had just proven itself a necessity, as she'd slipped trying to get out of the tub and into Jane's room for the phone.

Wondering if she could roll over, get her weight on her good leg, she rose slightly and made the effort. But when sharp pain whipped up and around like a tornado in her ankle, she collapsed.

What the hell was she going to do? Lie here all night like a fish? Maybe inch her way across the bathroom floor, down the hall and into—

Just then Mariah heard something. A crash. Downstairs. Wood splitting. She sucked air, and her pulse jumped in her blood. Not good. Robbery and incapacitated naked girl did not go well together.

She tried to work herself up into a sitting position, but her wrist and ankle hurt like hell, and she was slow.

There were footsteps on the stairs, a rustle outside the bathroom door. A thought poked into Mariah's brain—one she clung to for dear life. Jane. Maybe she'd forgotten something.

She called out, "Jane!" *I can't believe I'm about to say this.* "I've fallen and I can't get up."

"Do not be alarmed. I am here to help you."

Sick, gut-tight fear gripped Mariah, made her forget the pain screaming up her ankle.

Not Jane.

Had she locked the bathroom door?

"I have a knife and a baseball bat in here," she shouted, scanning the room for anything that resembled those two items. Emery board, toilet plunger… "And I'm not afraid to use them."

"I am sure that you could do great damage if provoked, but I am not here to hurt you, Miss Kennedy."

Was it Mr. Sexy Accent?

Mr. Next Door?

Oh my God.

"Don't come in here," she warned, more afraid of him seeing her naked than she was of him attacking her.

She was such an idiot.

"Miss Kennedy, I heard you scream." He was right outside the door now and probably unstoppable.

"I'm fine." She sounded embarrassingly hysterical. "Nothing's wrong. I just saw a mouse and—"

"I do not believe you."

The door squeaked open.

"Oh my God, don't come in here—"

He didn't listen. "Perhaps you need a doc—"

"Dammit!" Completely nude and in a most unflattering position, she tried to roll into the bath mat. "Get out. Get out."

"You are hurt."

"I'm also naked. Get out."

He went to her, knelt beside her. "I would never take advantage of such a situation."

She glared up at him. "I don't believe that for a minute."

A glimmer of humor lit his eyes. "Smart girl." He grabbed a towel and draped it over her. "But I give you my word this is no attempt at seduction, merely a rescue."

"I don't need to be rescued."

"I beg to differ."

"Listen, Mr. Fandal, this is my house and I want you to leave."

"Who will help you if I leave?"

"I'll think of someone or I'll get out of here myself."

"Crawling around on the floor like a lame pup?"

"Did you just call me a dog?"

Zayad gave an impatient groan, flashed his gaze to the ceiling. Never had he known a woman like this one—obstinate, headstrong, ready to injure herself further in the name of pride. He was not used to following the orders of others, but with her he felt it would be far more productive. "If you prefer to wallow in your mulishness, I shall stand behind the door in case you have need of me."

"No. Thank you. Seriously I appreciate the gesture, but you can leave. I'm fine."

He stood up, walked out of the bathroom and waited behind the door. "I shall stand behind the door until you realize you need my assistance."

She snorted. "Well, you'll be waiting all night for that, buddy."

Moments later he heard her groan with pain.

"Miss Kennedy?"

"I'm fine. Just fine."

Seconds later there was another cry of pain and a soft thud.

"Still fine, Miss Kennedy?"

"Yes."

He shook his head, walked back into the bathroom. "I do not enjoy playing games. You will not send me away again, and I will help you until more suitable help arrives."

"There is no suitable help."

"Your roommate is not home yet?"

"No."

"But she is returning soon, yes?"

"She's actually going to be out of town for a week teaching some Hollywood bimbo how to cook."

Alarm moved through Zayad. He had not heard her correctly. Jane gone for one week. Impossible. He had but two weeks to know her, make her understand her past, her family's history, see if she was ready to return to her homeland and take up her duties as princess. How could this happen? How could he have allowed his plan to be thwarted?

Frustration swam in his blood. What was he to do now? Follow her? Rent another home in Los Angeles for one week, then return to Ventura with her?

He glanced down at the woman who needed his assistance. With great care he eased her into his arms. He had to take care of this situation first and quickly, then find a solution to his woes with Jane.

Head against his chest, Mariah groaned. "This is so humiliating."

"What is? Falling down or being nude?"

"Oh, of course the naked part."

A grin tugged at his lips. "Miss Kennedy, you have nothing to feel ashamed of. Your body is beautiful, lush, and your skin is softer than silk. It took great effort to tear my gaze from you, but as you were hurt, I felt compelled to do so."

He watched her eyes widen and her lips part.

Chuckling, he lifted her up, bath mat and all, and headed out of the steamy room. "Praise be. I have found a way to keep you quiet."

Four

The pounding in her ankle aside, Mariah was still reeling from Mr. Next Door's compliment as he carried her down the stairs. She knew she shouldn't be reeling. In fact, she should have told him that his cheesy lines about her lushness and soft skin sucked and then given him a good slap.

But the thing was, she didn't want to think that what he'd said was a line. He'd looked at her with such devilishness, such sincerity, it had nearly had her wrapping her arms around his neck and demanding a kiss. And not just any kiss. From him she wanted open mouth, a little sweep of the tongue and maybe a nibble or two on her bottom lip.

Oh, it had been too long. She felt like an old, ratty plum on a tree, desperate to be picked, saved from a pruney future. Dangerous waters...

"Where are you taking me?" she asked him.

"To bed."

There it was—the deep end of those dangerous waters. "Mr. Fandal—"

"I think it is now appropriate for you to call me Zayad."

"And I'm thinking, after the whole bare-butt incident, it might be best to preserve some boundaries."

"And you think formality is the way to do this?"

Not a clue. "Let's not get off track here. We were talking about you taking me to bed."

"That's correct. Not to get undressed and join you, but so you may rest as I call the doctor."

She wilted—just slightly. "Oh." Not that she would allow herself to contemplate such a thing, but it sure would be nice to be wanted.

When he reached her bedroom, Zayad whipped back her white cotton sheets and placed her gently on the bed. "I will only be a moment," he informed her. "I must make a phone call to the doctor, then I will return."

"My doctor doesn't make house calls."

"No. But mine does."

"Yours?" She stared up into that rough, intense and highly sensual face and wondered just who this new neighbor of hers was. Had his own doctor on call—and at eight o'clock at night, no less—had a fancy accent, worldly expression, tailored clothes, highly intelligent eyes and was impressively quick with a comeback.

A stab of pain the size of New Jersey suddenly invaded her ankle. She dropped her cheek to the pillow, closed her eyes and moaned. When she opened her eyes again, Zayad was halfway out the door.

"Hey, Zayad?"

He turned. "Yes?"

"How did you know this was my room?"

A slow, almost fiendish smile drifted to his lips. "Careful deduction. You do not seem a risk taker to me, so the first-floor bedroom seemed correct."

Sad but true.

"And then there was your computer, law books and yellow legal pads." He pointed to her many Hockney posters littering the white walls. "The artwork. This is you."

The law books and such, she understood, but the artwork—that startled her. In all the time they were married, Alan had never even asked her about her love of Hockney, much less noticed if she had a connection to it. "Why is the art me?"

His gaze swept the room and he took a thoughtful breath. "Firstly, you live in a town that boasts a beach-like feel, as many of Hockney's paintings do. You are also very colorful, Mariah, and there is an interesting humor about you, as well."

She just stared at him. *He got all that in two meetings? Oh, yeah, this guy was dangerous all right.* "That was some pretty swift deducing from doorstep to backyard to bathroom to bedroom."

He grinned, haughtiness filling his black gaze. "I am said to be intuitive as well as highly intelligent."

"And maybe just a bit arrogant, too?" she added with a pained smirk.

"Oh, no, Mariah," he said without humor this time. "I am far more than a bit." And with that he turned and left.

Thirty minutes later, after a complete examination of her wrist and incredibly swollen ankle, the doctor—

who was so young Mariah wondered if he'd had his first shave yet—told her in the same accent as her neighbor's that her wrist was badly bruised. But her ankle?

"I am afraid it is a serious sprain," he said, his dark eyes on her. "I will prescribe a mild painkiller and bring you a brace and crutches. You may want an X-ray as well. In the meantime, you must rest. You will need to remain off your foot for a few days."

Mariah shook her head. "I can't stay in bed. I have a ton of work to do."

"Work that will have to be done from bed, young lady."

She had to bite her tongue to keep from laughing. The twelve-year-old doctor had actually called her "young lady." "I'm an attorney and I have a huge case to prepare. Lives are at stake and all that," she said, trying to appeal to him in a way he'd understand. "If I can't get up and get to work, I can forget about court in three weeks, and getting a wonderful mother of two custody and child support."

The doctor tried to look sympathetic. "I understand, Miss Kennedy. But if you want your ankle to heal, you will do as I say. And you will need someone to help you."

Zayad turned to her. "Your roommate is returning—"

"In a week."

His lips thinned. "Do you have a friend to help you?"

"Not really." Jane was her best friend. She'd allowed no one to get close to her since Alan. Of course, she had her work colleagues, but no one who she'd feel comfortable asking for help.

"Family?" Zayad asked.

Mariah shook her head.

"A man?" asked the doctor.

Heat rushed Mariah's cheeks. "No. No man."

Zayad felt relieved at the news, though he did not wish to examine why. He had more important matters to see to than his attraction to this woman, such as seeing to his sister.

Beside him Mariah shifted on the bed. She looked so beautiful, so soft and needful, lying there still draped in her large white towel, her legs exposed. It took all he had to force his mind to shut down, to remind his body that it would be foolish to climb in beside her, remove that towel and explore.

She was injured, and he had to think of his mission.

Right now he should be following his sister to Los Angeles, finding out about her passions and pursuits, as he should have done so many years ago. He should be telling her the truth. But he had given it much thought on the way to get the doctor and he knew that wouldn't be wise. He would look like a stalker, following her from Los Angeles back to Ventura, and he would never get the answers he needed.

Mariah looked up, found his gaze.

Answers Jane Hefner's best friend might be able to reveal as she recovered from her injury.

Zayad paused, his mind circling a new path.

He was no nursemaid, but his need to uncover the truth about his sister and her past and present could force his hand—could draw him in to Mariah Kennedy's world for a few days.

An interesting, though risky prospect.

He turned to Dr. Adair, the son of his physician in Emand. "I will care for the girl myself."

Adair's eyes went wide. "Your— Sir, I do not think…"

"It is done," Zayad said swiftly.

"Excuse me?" Mariah fairly sputtered.

Zayad continued speaking to Adair. "I live next door. I will cook for her, bathe her—"

"Are you certain that is wise, sir?"

"I am." His answer was firm, unmovable, and the doctor nodded.

"Excuse me." Mariah actually sat up, her anger evident in those beautiful tiger's eyes and irritated tone. "First of all, I'm not a girl. And second of all, there'll be no bathing by anyone other than me."

Zayad began, "I was merely suggesting that I remain on hand to assist—"

"I don't need any extra hands," she uttered through pain.

"I am afraid you do, Miss Kennedy." The doctor eased a brown brace that resembled a boot over her foot and ankle and set the Velcro straps in place. "As I said, you must remain in bed, off that ankle for at least two days. If Mr. Fandal does not help, who will?"

She opened her mouth, then promptly shut it. What a question. And one that made her feel like a gigantic loser. Seriously, Jane was gone and Mariah couldn't ask her to come home—not with that kind of money at stake.

Mariah frowned, winced. Her ankle hurt. Dammit! There really was no one who could come to her rescue. Except…she lifted her lids, found his black gaze, and her belly softened and warmed.

"Why in the world would you want to do this?" she asked him. "You hardly know me."

Zayad sat beside her on the bed. Behind him Dr. Adolescence discreetly left the room.

"Have you never felt compelled to help a stranger in need, Mariah?" he asked.

Every day of her life since she'd climbed out of the depression-coma her ex had sent her reeling into after he'd not only cheated on her with his fitness instructor but also had announced he wanted to marry the woman. From that day on she'd felt compelled to help others in similar situations—hopeless and alone and without much in the way of funds. She'd gone back to school, passed the bar with flying colors and opened up her own practice a few months later.

She dropped back against the pillows and sighed. "After our conversation tonight in the yard, I think you know I fight for the underdog. And I bet you can also guess that it's become a passion of mine."

A passion Mariah had hoped would help her heal a little with each case she took and won. Sad thing was, she didn't think she *had* healed all that much.

"I will see the doctor to the door," Zayad told her. "And when I return, we will talk about dinner, yes?"

"Listen," she said as he stood up. "I'm sorry if this seems ungrateful, because I really do appreciate what you're trying to do—"

"But?"

"But I don't trust you."

"I understand."

She lifted herself up on her elbows. "You do?"

"It is your nature."

"It's my past," she corrected.

He nodded.

She said, "You're clearly after something here, and I don't know if it's me or Jane or if it's a way of repenting for some horrible sin you've committed, but know this—I'll be watching you like a hawk."

Sensuality fairly dripped from his smile. "I would expect nothing less from you, Mariah."

She swallowed thickly. "Good."

"Incidentally, the only sin I cannot seem to shake is continually wanting the one thing I definitely should not have." His grin widened as his gaze flickered to the white towel she held firmly to her breasts. "But I will never repent."

Lust ripped through Mariah's core at his words. The pain in her ankle was nothing to it.

She watched him walk out her bedroom door, leaving an aura of irrepressible and highly erotic male in his wake. For the past four years she'd often wondered if she might be dead from the waist down. But now she knew the truth. She was alive and well and tingling and hot and she wanted to feel a man on her skin again.

But not just any man.

She closed her eyes and inhaled.

That man.

And the knowledge scared her to death.

Five

"**Y**ou have done what?"

Standing at the kitchen counter, a can of soup in his hand, a cell phone tucked between his ear and shoulder, Zayad tried to explain to his brother the realities of this strange situation he had found himself in tonight. "I have agreed to care for our sister's roommate until she is back on her feet."

Sakir snorted. "This is madness. You know nothing about care. You cannot cook, clean, make small talk. She will see through you in an instant."

"Perhaps, but she has little choice in the matter. She has no other help. Her family is deceased, her friend is gone and…she has no man."

"No man?" Sakir said all too slowly, a reminder that he still lived most of the year in Texas. "You say this as though it pleases you."

"I having no feeling either way."

"I do not believe you, brother. Seduction is on your brain, I sense it. Is she pleasing to look at?"

A flash of heat moved through Zayad. He found the feeling most disconcerting. "She is blond and small with heavenly curves. Her eyes are the color of Emand's softest sand and her lips the color of wine. She is far more than pleasing, my brother. But—"

"But? There should be no reason for you not to—"

"She is an American and I am Sultan. That is reason enough, but I will give you more. She is angry at something or someone, and I feel in no mood to soften her." He opened a cabinet and grabbed a blue bowl. "No matter how strong my desire might be, I am only staying here to gather information—"

"Staying there? In her home?" Sakir roared with laughter.

The bowl dropped from Zayad's hand into the sink with a loud crash. He barked at his brother. "It is the only way to ensure that my mission is successful. I must be around her to acquire information. I have but two weeks to learn all I can about our sister, and then I must return to Emand."

"The mission, yes. It must be the most important thing." Sakir switched gears for a moment. "You will not return to Emand without another stop in Texas, as promised?"

"Of course. But it is only to see your beautiful wife."

"Rita is looking forward to it, although she is a bit under the weather."

"Your son or daughter is already causing their mother trouble, yes?"

Sakir chuckled, light and familiar. The sound bore into Zayad's hardened heart. He missed his brother greatly. Their friendship. Their battles, both verbal and with sword. And now, with the talk of family so prevalent as of late—his sister, his son and Sakir's child on the way—Zayad wanted nothing more than to have his entire clan together, safe, under one roof. If that were only possible.

"Do you want me to come to California?"

Zayad smiled at his brother's offer while he grabbed something Fandal had called a "can's opener" from the drawer. "No. You should not leave your wife just now. You will meet our sister soon enough. And besides, two sheikhs would surely stand out in this small town."

Sakir laughed. "Indeed."

Zayad cursed as large droplets of chicken broth hit the floor.

"What is it?" Sakir asked.

"I am attempting to open a can of something called 'chicken and stars soup.' It's my patient's favorite."

"You are not actually cooking?"

"I am," Zayad replied indignantly.

"Why not get one of the servants to see to the meal?"

Zayad leaned over the sink and turned on the faucet. Water shot into the sink. "I must act as a normal man."

"A normal man would have called a pizzeria by now."

Again Zayad cursed. "I must go. I have added too much water to this mess."

Zayad ignored his brother's laughter and hung up the phone. He had battled lions, six warriors at one time and the fiercest of swordsmen, he could see to one simple meal. He only had to concentrate.

Ten minutes later he walked into Mariah's bedroom. The clock on the wall chimed nine. A little late for dinner, but she had claimed she had not eaten a thing since noon and had looked very pale when he had left her.

On a tray he had found under the kitchen sink Zayad had placed the watery soup, some cheese, a slice of anemic-looking bread, a second pain pill, a glass of water and a glass of wine for himself.

He stopped just before the bed, tray still in hand, and took in the sight before him. She was sitting up, white blanket tucked in at her waist. She looked young, her face free of makeup and frustration. Her long, blond hair hung loose. She had put on the robe he had brought her, and at first glance he thought it very prim and proper. But at second glance he noticed that its white fabric was fairly thin. He could see the outline of her breasts through the cotton.

An invisible vise gripped his chest as he stared. She was no practiced seductress, sitting there in her virginal white world, but to him she could not be more disturbingly sexy.

He placed the tray on her lap, and fought his roguish impulse to catch a closer look at what lay beneath that flimsy robe.

He lost the fight.

The robe gaped slightly at the chest, and he could not help but see one slope of full breast, one rise of pink nipple.

His groin tightened painfully and he moved away, fell back into a chair beside the bed. He was surprised by his lack of restraint. Surprised and bothered.

"Thank you for this," she said, placing the napkin in

her lap. "I may not show it, but I really appreciate your help."

He crossed his arms over his chest. "Wait until after you have tasted the soup before thanking me. I am afraid I am not much of a chef."

"I'm sure it's great. I can't cook, either. I can barely nuke a hot dog without incident." She picked up her spoon. "The cooking is Jane's department. She's a genius."

"Is she in food preparation?" As if he did not know.

"She's a professional chef. Works downtown at an Italian restaurant. She should have her own restaurant already, but, you know, money is always an issue."

He did not know, but he nodded anyway.

She took a bite of cheese and asked, "What is it you do, Zayad?"

It was the answer he had always longed to give. Impractical and unbecoming a sultan. But quite right here. "I am in art. Collecting, preserving, then selling if the buyer is right."

"Really? Well, that explains the Hockney thing. Do you collect paintings? Sculpture?"

"Swords, actually."

"Swords." Her bite of cheese fell back on the plate. "As in slice and dice, battles, *Braveheart*—those kinds of swords?"

An amused smile played on his lips. "In my country swords are revered. Even swordplay is considered an art form, a sport. Like fencing. Boys as young as five are taught the art of swordplay."

She picked up her spoon, looking a little uneasy.

"And to think, LEGOs and monster trucks are as far as most American five-year-old boys get with play and sport. What country are you from?"

"A little place you probably have never heard of."

"Try me."

"It is called Emand."

"Nope, never heard of it." She smiled—a smile wide and open and just a little teasing—and it was the first time Zayad had seen her without a mask of acerbity. With the mask she was beautiful, but without it she was stunning, irresistible.

Would she fight him if he kissed her?

He imagined she would.

"What is your country like?" she asked.

He sighed, his mind falling away from seduction to his homeland. "It is magical, beautiful, yet still a little wild."

"Wild, huh? The deserts or the people?" She looked down her nose at him. "The men don't drag the women around by their hair or anything, do they?"

"The ruler of Emand abolished the ways of the caveman long ago." When she smiled, he did, too. "The truth is while some choose to follow the ancient, more traditional ways, most of the women in my country are educated, feministic and have no qualms about telling their men what is on their mind."

"I like this ruler of yours."

And he likes you.

Aloud he said, "And what of you? I know that you are an attorney. What I do not know is why you seem so on edge, full of tension."

"You mean stressed out?"

"This sounds appropriate, yes."

She paused, stared at him, then sighed and shook her head. "I have a case that's not going very well. I tried to get the parties to settle out of court, resolve their issues without involving a long legal battle, but the ex-husband won't agree. Now I'm trying to find information that will help my client win." She gestured to her ankle. "And look what I have to contend with."

"What is the case?"

"Child custody."

"In specifics, Miss Kennedy," he said with a grin. "Do you really want to know?"

"I would not ask if I was not interested."

In between small sips of soup, she explained. "The woman I'm defending was a wonderful wife and mother for fourteen years. Her husband was verbally abusive, had numerous affairs. He didn't want to spend time with his kids. They've been divorced for about a month now, and she got custody of the kids. A few weeks ago she met a man and has been dating him. Well, the ex-husband heard about this and flipped out—though he has a girlfriend." She sighed, put down her spoon. "He's suing for full custody of the kids. Kids he couldn't care less about. My client never asked for alimony. She didn't want anything from him for herself, just child support for the kids. But the husband's pride has been nicked. His affairs never came up in court, and now he's claiming he was a faithful, devoted husband and father and she was the slut and that his kids shouldn't be around a mother like that."

Zayad's jaw was rigid. He detested men like this one—cowards. "He wants to use the children as revenge."

"Exactly. This guy is rich and powerful and has no trail for his affairs that his ex-wife or I could find. The women aren't talking. His friends and business associates aren't talking. The hotel and flower receipts my client had found have suddenly vanished."

"There is always a way to recover these things."

"I've tried. She's tried. Nothing." She nibbled on the bread. "I don't want to lose this case."

The male protector inside Zayad sprang to life, and he made an imprudent vow. "You will not lose."

"I have a killer sprain and no way to do any legwork on this case."

"We will find this man's trail."

Her eyes narrowed with surprise. "We?"

He moved from the chair to her bedside. "This case reminds me of my own struggles. I, too, had to fight to reclaim a child from a parent who only wished to use him."

"What are you talking about? What child?"

"Mine. I have a son."

Mariah's mouth dropped open. "You do?"

"You do not see me as parental?"

"Well, no." She shook her head, felt cruel for saying something like that. "What I mean is that, well, you're so…"

"What?"

"I don't know." *Gorgeous, charming, cultured.* The men she knew with those traits were usually the kind of men she fought in court. The kind of men who wanted to get rid of their baggage—wife, kids—and start fresh. Her mind whirled. This man had a child? This man had fought for his child? "I don't know what to make of you, Zayad."

He leaned toward her, brushed a stray lock of hair behind her ear. "It was falling in the soup."

He didn't move away. He stayed close, his mouth just inches from hers. She felt his warmth, and her heart jumped her in chest. "It's really bad soup, by the way," she whispered.

His gaze moved over her face, pausing at her lips. "I did warn you."

Mariah paused, let those words sink in, cool her heated skin. She couldn't believe herself. She actually had been ready to kiss him, throw her arms around his neck and go for it. This man she hardly knew. This man who represented everything that terrified her in a lover.

She swallowed hard. "I'd better get some sleep. That last pain pill is starting to wear off."

For a moment he remained, deliciously close and still tempting. Then his gaze flickered and he pulled back, a vein in his temple pulsating. "If you need anything, I will be in the living area."

Her heart dropped into her belly. "*My* living room?"

He nodded. "On the couch."

"The couch." Just outside her bedroom door? Him in his boxers, or whatever he wore to bed, on her couch, in her living room?

"This is all right, yes?" he asked, standing. "If you need assistance in the night."

"Yes, of course," she sputtered.

"Good night then."

"'Night," she called after him. "And again, thanks."

When he left, she fell back on the pillow and sighed. Oh, what she had to be missing right now. The feeling of his face so close to her own had been heaven. She could just imagine that a kiss would be absolute magic.

Just the thought had her body glowing, had her senses high and heady with a feeling she hadn't wanted to feel ever again—a feeling that made her vulnerable.

Pure, unadulterated lust.

"Well, I'm here," Jane said over the phone ten minutes later. "The house is enormous and the actress is anorexic, but she seems pretty into the cooking lessons so—" She paused. "Wait, what's wrong?"

"What makes you think something's wrong?" Mariah asked, kicking off her covers with her good leg and reaching for the wine Zayad hadn't touched.

"You haven't interjected or snorted when I said the anorexic thing. What's going on?"

After a healthy swallow of wine, she admitted, "Well, there is something."

"I knew it. Spill."

"Funny you should say that word, because after you left today, I took a bath. And, well, I sort of had a spill when I tried to get out."

"Oh my God, are you okay?"

She thought about telling Jane the truth, but didn't want her running home to help. "It's just a sprain. I'm fine—if you don't count the fifteen minutes of humiliation I had to endure."

"What's there to be humiliated about? You fell—"

"Naked. I fell naked. And I was lying on our ratty bath mat totally naked when Mr. Gorgeous from next door heard me scream and busted in like a superhero to help me."

"You're lying!"

"Do I sound like I'm lying?"

"Wow. So then what?"

Another swallow of wine. "So, then he picked me up and put me in my bed, called his doctor and then proceeded to tell me that he's staying with me until you get back."

"I'll be home in two hours." Panic dripped in Jane's voice.

"No," Mariah said firmly. "Me and my bum ankle are not coming between you and your restaurant money."

"Forget that. You've got a stranger taking care of you."

"No. It's fine. He's fine. He's actually…" Mariah set the empty wineglass on her bedside table and reveled in the decadent relaxation she felt.

"Actually what, M?" Jane asked.

"A pretty nice guy if you ignore the killer looks, arrogant and opinionated attitude and irresistible mouth."

"Oh, really?" Jane said, a wide grin in her tone. "Well, good for you. It's about time."

"No, no, no. Nothing like that. If anything, he's into you. Whenever we have a conversation, the subject always seems to come back to you."

"I don't know why. I've never met the guy." Jane paused, then said, "So, are you sure I shouldn't come home?"

"You stay with the stick-figure actress and make a ton of money. I'll be good."

"Oh, for once I hope not."

Mariah grimaced, feeling tired and ready to crash. "'Night, Jane."

"'Night."

Mariah hung up the phone and without much thought popped a pain pill. Her mind was on her new roomie and his sexy bod on her old, plaid couch.

Sigh.

Maybe Jane should have come home, if only to protect Mariah against her own messed-up feelings. But Jane had been doing that for four years now. Wasn't it time Mariah protected herself?

Without an answer Mariah turned off the light and settled into the pillows, hoping sleep would soon seize her mind.

Zayad heard her get up and checked his watch.

Twenty minutes past one in the morning.

He hadn't been to sleep yet. Could not sleep, in fact. As he tried to maintain a semicomfortable position on the thin and frustratingly short couch, his mind rumbled with activity. Though not on the subject it should be on. No, he was thinking about the softness of his patient's cheek, the scent of her skin, the hunger in her eyes. She had made him weak with just a look, and he would wrestle a king snake for another moment such as that one.

How was he to stop himself from making love to her? How was he to remember his mission here if the one woman who held the key to that mission also held the key to a new and boundless pleasure?

Behind him he heard her shuffle in, the roughness of the boot brace apparent on the wood floors.

He sat up, turned to look at her. "Miss Kennedy?"

She gasped. Her hand flew to her throat and she said a little too loudly, "You scared the life out of me."

"I apologize."

She gripped the window ledge to hold herself steady as she stared at him. She looked like a beautiful phantom in the pale yellow light of the street lamp outside, and Zayad had to force himself to stay on the couch instead of going to her and pulling her into his arms. "What are you doing out of bed?"

She shook her head. "Nothing."

"Then let me help you back." He knew it was a mistake to go to her, but there was nothing for it. She needed his help.

She sagged against the window, her thin robe gripping at the chest, her eyes and head hanging down.

"Are you all right?" he asked.

"I don't really know. I'm kinda out of it."

He tilted her chin up, made her gaze meet his. "Did you take more than one pain pill?"

She shook her head vigorously. "Nope. But I did have your wine."

"That was not a wise decision."

She gave him a mock frown, perhaps mimicking his own, then she pushed away from the window and leaned into him. "I wouldn't normally say this, but I find you very attractive."

He smiled, could not help himself. "Thank you, Miss Kennedy. I find you very attractive, as well."

"No 'Miss Kennedy.' I'm not a schoolteacher, for heaven's sake." She let her head fall against his chest. "But I think I've become a nun. Maybe you should call me Sister Mariah."

"I do not think so."

She looked up, her tiger's eyes warm and vulnerable. "What would you call me, then?"

He touched her face, his thumb moving over her cheekbone. "I would call you alive and desirable and filled with a hunger that needs to be satiated or—"

"Or I'll wilt."

"It is possible."

She sighed. "I know. I know. I've been celibate for too long."

"You need sleep, Mariah. Let me take you back to bed."

"No." Her eyes on his, she grazed her lower lip with her teeth and said, "I think I'm going to kiss you."

Zayad said nothing, just held her as she looked completely ready for his mouth on hers. He could not allow this, not in her state of mind. After all, he was no scoundrel. At least, he tried hard not to be.

No, he should not allow this.

But he did not have a choice as she fell against him, her arms wrapping around his neck, her fingers threading in his hair. With just a wisp of a smile she pressed his head down to hers and kissed him. It was unlike him, but he let her lead him, let her take the control and the pleasure that her body needed.

She sighed and tilted her head to reach him better as her fingers fisted in his hair. Zayad tried to slow his heart, ease the tightness in his chest, but it was not easy. Her kiss was slow and sensual, wet lips and soft tongue. He could not restrain himself. He nipped at her bottom lip, pressed his groin into her belly.

With great effort, Mariah eased back for a moment. Her eyes were liquid as she said, "I haven't done that in years."

Zayad stilled, his arms around her. Years? That could

not be true. It was not possible that this striking female could go years without being kissed by a man.

Her eyes drifted closed, then opened, then closed, and Zayad knew she was starting to fade. Shifting his position, he gathered her in his arms and lifted her up.

Her head promptly fell against his shoulder as he carried her into the bedroom. "You will sleep late tomorrow, Mariah."

"No," she murmured. "Tomorrow I have to visit Mama Tara."

"Your mother?" Zayad said, confused. "I thought you said you had no relatives to care for you—"

"She's not my real mother."

Zayad thought it best not to ask her any more questions. She was exhausted and on a combination of pain medication and wine. It was time for her to sleep.

He laid her on the bed and tucked the covers under her chin. But she did not fall asleep immediately. She looked up at him, gave him a melancholy smile.

"You see, my parents died when I was twelve. My grandma raised me until I was eighteen, then she died, too. While she was alive, she wasn't all that active, so my best friend's mother—Tara—took me under her wing. She treated me like a daughter and she was every bit the mother to me."

Shock bit him, made him feel slow and detached from time and the room. "Your best friend?"

"Jane."

His gut clenched with tension. Could she be speaking of the same Tara? "Where is this woman now?"

Mariah closed her eyes, let her head drift to the side. "She lives in Ojai, at a beautiful facility there."

"Facility. She is not ill?" He asked questions he knew the answers to. But he had to be certain.

"No. She's blind."

Zayad's throat went dry. Yes, this was Tara.

Before he had seen the pictures that his investigators had supplied, he had built up an image of his father's American lover—wild and interested only in power and a rich lover. He had thought her like his son's mother. But in those photographs her face had shown none of these traits. Though he would see for himself.

"You will visit Tara tomorrow," he told Mariah.

Mariah's lashes lifted and she stared at him, groggy and very beautiful in the moon's light. "But how? That infant doctor of yours—"

"I will take you myself."

"He said I have to stay in bed for two days."

"He wanted you off your foot. You will be off your foot."

Her eyes narrowed lazily. "You're taking care of me, helping me with my next case and driving me to Tara's. What is it you want from me?"

He did not answer her query, but on his way out of the room said, "Get some rest. We will leave at nine."

Six

Her pride hurt as much as her ankle the next morning.

Mariah sat in the passenger side of Zayad's black SUV as they raced up the 101 freeway. Her seat was slightly reclined and her booted ankle rested on a stack of pillows. Zayad had meant for her to be comfortable, but it was a lost cause. All she wanted to do was fade into the gray leather seats. She remembered everything that had happened last night, from her wine-induced rest on the window ledge to Zayad putting a gentlemanly arm around her waist to his not-so-gentlemanly kiss a moment later.

That last bit made her smile, so she turned to look out the window at the orange groves. Who was she trying to kid? Zayad may have kissed her back with double the heat and intensity of any man she'd ever known, but she'd been the instigator. She'd told him he looked mighty fine with her eyes, then gone in for the kill.

Damn that wine and pain medicine. They'd totally messed her up. She shouldn't be acting like a teenager anymore. She glanced over at Zayad, took in his chiseled features and those amazing, teasing, oh-so-full lips she'd felt last night. What did he think of her? He hadn't mentioned their make-out session last night or when he'd seen her this morning, and she couldn't read his eyes. With looks like that, maybe he was used to forward women.

Or, on the opposite end of the spectrum, maybe he hadn't really wanted to kiss her last night. Maybe he'd just been laying on the pity for the poor drugged-up cripple girl.

She mentally groaned.

Can I get any more pathetic?

Her gaze slipped from his face down to his neck, then lower still. Along with those amazing lips, she'd felt his chest and arms. Hard as steel and corded with muscle. Too bad he'd covered them up today, she thought, giving in to the thoughts of her wanton-woman alter ego. But his clothes did flatter what he had in spades. Tan pants that showed off his tight backside to perfection and a crisp white shirt open at the nape. If she wasn't so reclined, she mused, she could probably have a nice look at that muscle.

She frowned and shifted in the leather bucket seat. She needed to get her mind out of the proverbial gutter and onto something safer.

Casually she glanced around. "This is a nice car."

"Thank you."

"You must sell a lot of those swords."

A muscle twitched in his jaw. "They are very popular."

"I'm sure they are."

"There are many who enjoy a beautiful blade."

"Of course. So, why come to Ventura to work, then? Wouldn't Los Angeles be a better—"

"A better what?"

"Well, not better but a more lucrative place to collect pieces and sell them? Lots of stars and eccentric people who would be interested in adding a sword to their eclectic art collections?"

He glanced over at her, haughtiness in his gaze. "Do you feel life is only about gain, about money?"

The question made her laugh. This was the first time in her life she'd been accused of such a thing. "Of course not. Look at the work that I do."

He shrugged. "Perhaps you do such work for more than just altruistic reasons."

"What do you mean by that?"

"I do not know. I do not know your past or what drives your decisions now, but the way you speak of men, of winning for your clients, it is—"

"It's personal, Mr. Fandal," she interrupted, her words sounding far too tight.

Zayad said nothing to this and she stared past him to the ocean. Wild and inviting yet a bit intimidating at times. And the sand, soft and steady. Zayad had seen her soft last night, had seen the woman in her and not just the acerbic machine-for-hire she was at work. Perhaps he'd liked what he'd seen. Now the severe woman he'd met on the doorstep had returned. Normally at a moment like this, with an encounter that had nothing to do with work, she'd tuck her tail between her legs and retreat.

Her gaze flickered toward him. "Look, I didn't mean to jump on you—"

He turned, eyes suddenly filled with humor.

She laughed, a little shyly at first. "You know what I mean." She paused, then lifted her hands in mock surrender. "The thing is, you're right. I have some stuff in my past that drives most of my decisions today. But honestly I believe my reasons for doing what I do are altruistic in nature." *At least I hope so.* The afterthought alarmed her, so she decided not to examine it. She chose to return to a familiar subject.

"So, back to the beginning of this conversation. Ventura, California. Why?"

"Would it be too poetic to say that the ocean is a welcome tonic to my wearied senses?"

She followed along. "And that the glitz and glamour of Hollywood would bore you to tears, make you long for the simpler life?"

"Exactly." He grinned, gave her a wink. "I think you understand me, Miss Kennedy."

"Oh, for heaven's sake, let's drop the 'Miss.' I'm Mariah and you're—"

"Yes? Who am I?"

You're too gorgeous, too generous, too interesting and way too irresistible. "I think I'll save that answer until I know you better."

"And you are planning on knowing me better?"

There was a racehorse inside her chest thump, thump, thumping along, but she managed to say, "Well, since we're sort of stuck together, I don't know what choice I have…"

The corners of his mouth lifted in one sexy smile. "I like this…stuck together."

God help her, so did she. She turned and faced forward. She could hardly feel the ache in her ankle anymore. The ache in her heart, breasts and core had drowned out the pain.

This Ojai…

Around and around they drove, up the mountain and through the towns, with no security trailing behind—as he had instructed.

Zayad could not help but feel drawn to this spot. There were shades of Emand here, particularly the sultan's palace gardens. Fruit trees, perfect lawns and a sky so intense a blue, he wondered for a moment if he were at home.

He grinned. All that was missing were the golden sands.

He did not glance to his right, but knew he had his golden sands beside him. They dwelled in Mariah's eyes. Eyes that had haunted him through a painfully sleepless night. Eyes that had drawn him to that soft mouth, that pink tongue, that taste of wine and mystery.

"I love coming up here," Mariah said, ripping Zayad from his thoughts. "It's so different than the beachy areas, you know?"

Zayad pulled onto Main Street. "The mountains are beautiful, as are the pear and walnut trees."

"It's really peaceful. I'd love to move my practice up here sometime. Maybe get a horse."

"You like to ride?"

"I do. I'm not great at it, but I love the feeling of animal and person being one."

Horse and rider—one being. Zayad had said this many times. His gaze swept over her fitted white sundress. Yes, she would love his country.

"And of course," she continued, "I would love being closer to Tara."

Ah, yes, Zayad mused, his mood darkening slightly. The reason he had come here today. Tara. "What of Jane? Does she want to be near her mother, as well?"

The mention of Jane brought a slight frown to Mariah's lips. "Of course she does. She's tried to get a chef's job here, but the competition is stiff and the money's worse. That's why she's working so hard. She's trying to save enough cash to open her own restaurant up here."

Not if he had anything to say on the matter. Jane was an Emand princess. She need not work if she did not want to. And if she did, no door would be closed to her, and money would be no object. But she would be in Emand, not Ojai.

He turned back to Mariah. "If Jane moved here, where would that leave you?"

"What?"

"She is your closest friend, yes?"

Mariah paused, felt a sudden tug at her heart. She swallowed hard. "She's my best friend."

"And you have no lover, correct?"

"We've already covered this, haven't we?"

He chuckled. "We have."

"And that's by choice, by the way."

"Yes, of course. But my point is this—if your friend moves, where does that leave you?"

She shrugged and fastened on her ol' reliable tough-cookie attitude—the one that was complete BS but made her feel in control and less like a loser. "That leaves me alone, I guess."

"And this is good for you?"

"I don't see you with a wife and a boatload of friends by your side. Must be good for you, too."

He took a moment in answering. "Yes, but alas..."

"Alas what?"

"A man can do very well—"

"Don't even go there, buddy." She pointed her finger at him. "Don't even say that a man is programmed to wander the earth alone, never needing to fully bond with one person. And that a woman requires a mate to be happy and fulfilled."

He shrugged. "All right, I will not say it—but only because I could not say the words as well as you just have." He grinned.

She wanted to toss him a huge frown, maybe a little sneer if she could muster it, but nothing negative sprouted from her heart. And even more annoying, she couldn't stop the smile that tugged at her lips. The guy was clever and drop-dead handsome and he made her weak—in more ways than one. She shook her head. "I think I'm not meant to find true happiness with someone. I don't believe in happily ever after anymore and I don't believe in soul mates."

"Neither do I. I have always been happiest when I am alone."

Why did that admission sadden her so much when her own had filled her with confidence?

He continued to say, "But I have never met a woman who also felt this way."

"Surprises you, huh?"

"Very much." His gaze moved over her. "You have been nothing but surprising to me, Mariah."

Her belly twisted and warmed under his gaze, and she turned to face the road. They were only about a block away from Tara's place. Good thing, too. If Mariah didn't watch her step, instead of telling him she was going to kiss him, she'd be coaxing him into the backseat of this truck.

She took a deep breath and said, "Turn at the next light."

The apartment the assisted-living coordinator showed them into was painted in bright, bold colors, and Zayad thought it interesting that a woman without sight lived in such a vivid atmosphere. The furniture was more of the same—a menagerie of red and gold and blue pieces, though all looked comfortable and at home in the rather small space.

Zayad's gaze shifted and he noticed a potter's wheel was set up in one corner of the room, facing a set of charming French doors, where a cool breeze floated in.

When the aide left, Zayad gestured to the wheel and asked Mariah, now ensconced on the red couch, "Who is the artist?"

"Tara is."

"She does not share this room with another?"

"Nope."

"But how would she work…?"

"She is an amazing woman." Mariah smiled at Zayad with eyes that read, "Just wait until you meet her." "She lets nothing stop her—especially when she wants something badly enough."

He wanted to remark that Tara sounded like a wonderful, brave and interesting woman, but he felt he would wait to meet the woman first.

"I have guests."

The cheerful, husky tone came from the doorway. Zayad looked up in time to see a tall, slim, long-legged woman in her midfifties with short blond hair streaked with an attractive pale gray. She wore a flowing orange dress with beaded earrings to match. She was very beautiful, but there was far more to her than her looks. This was a woman who was overflowing with life, happiness and an open spirit. Zayad understood at once why his father had been drawn to this woman.

Tara thrust her hands to her hips. "Where's my lovely Mariah? Why isn't she running over here to greet me?"

"I would run over to you, Tara," said Mariah, her eyes bright with the warmth one felt for someone they loved greatly. "I hurt my ankle last night."

Hearing her voice brought Tara straight to Mariah. She sat beside Mariah on the couch, fumbled just a bit for her hand. "It is of no importance. You came, my little one, that's what matters. Now, what's wrong with your ankle?"

"It's just a little bruise." Mariah glanced up at Zayad and smiled. "No worries."

Tara feigned gruffness. "It is my right to worry about you."

Mariah laughed. "I know."

"So, you didn't drive yourself up here, did you?" Tara turned, tilted her chin and faced Zayad. "Who have you brought with you?"

Zayad stepped back, feeling strange and slightly uncomfortable at how easily she had found him.

"How did you…?" Mariah laughed. "Of course."

Of course? What, of course? He had made no sound, no movement, no indication that he was in the room. He wanted to know what the mystery was.

"This is my neighbor," Mariah explained. "And… well, friend. He graciously offered to bring me up here even though I've been a real pain in the neck to him."

"Ah, my girl, your spirit is your charm." Tara stood, walked straight to Zayad and extended her hand. "Is it not?"

Zayad took her hand. "It is."

Her brows drew together. "Does this friend have a name?"

Zayad bent and kissed her hand. "My name is Zayad."

Confusion, then an unmistakable shadow of alarm moved across Tara's features and she eased her hand from his. All warmth, confidence and animation seemed to melt away from her expression, and Zayad wondered how well she had known her lover. Had she known of his family? His children's names?

It seemed she did.

"Are you two hungry?" Tara asked, recovering quickly and turning away from him.

"A little," Mariah said.

"Good. I'll go and get our lunch, then we can have a nice chat. I can't wait to hear what's been going on with you. And of course, finding out more about your new neighbor and what he's doing so far from home."

"Can I help you, Mrs. Hefner?" Zayad asked.

She headed into the other room. "No, thank you."

When they were alone again, Mariah turned to him. "That was a nice offer. But she likes to do these things herself. Oh, and it's not 'Mrs.' She was never married. Actually I think she was over-the-top in love with Jane's dad and couldn't bear to think of another man after he left her."

In love. Zayad bristled.

"What's wrong?" Mariah asked, watching him.

He shook his head. "I was thinking about this man leaving her."

"Yeah. What a jerk, huh?"

"How is it you know this?"

"Jane told me."

Black fury ignited in Zayad's belly at his father's foolish aide. For his sister to think that her own father did not want her—it was despicable. Even though Zayad's son came from a mother who only wanted to see gold, Zayad had only told him good things about Meyaan and that she did not come to see him because she was not well, but that she loved him a great deal.

"To not even want to know your own child." Mariah shook her head. "Horrible."

"Perhaps he did not know he had a child."

Mariah's face contorted with dismay. "What makes you say that?"

He could not answer, nor did he want to, as Tara rejoined them. She carried a platter laden with food. "My cold lemon chicken, potato salad and biscuits."

Zayad helped her with the platter and the serving until they were ready to eat. As they sat around a small iron table in a tiny though peaceful yard overlooking the mountainside, Tara spoke mostly to Mariah. She wanted to know all about her upcoming case and what her strategy was. When Mariah mentioned that Zayad was going to help her, Tara put down her uneaten biscuit on her plate full of uneaten food and faced him. "So, where are you from, Zayad?"

She knew exactly—he could see it on her face—but he replied anyway. "From a small country called Emand."

Sadness etched her features. "And is it a beautiful place? Ripe with olive groves and fig trees? Scented with spice and the warm sand at sunset?"

"It is." His father had told her much, and he almost felt badly for her.

"Sounds like you've been there, Tara," Mariah remarked, using the table to get herself into a standing position and grab her crutches.

"Perhaps in my mind," Tara said softly.

"Where are you going?" Zayad asked Mariah.

"The little girls' room to freshen up." She grinned. "Wanna come?"

"I will help you there, of course."

After Zayad had helped Mariah to the bathroom and told her to call for him when she was ready, he returned to the table and to Tara.

"Could you pass me a lump of that sugar, Zayad," she said. "As you have probably surmised by now, I cannot see well."

He did as she requested, watched as she placed the sugar in her glass of lemonade. "I think you see very well, madam."

"Thank you. I work very hard for normalcy." She smiled in his direction. "As Mariah has probably told you, I wasn't always blind. The furnishings you see around you have been with me for ages, and five years ago, when my sight began to wane, the comfort of being able to still detect color helped me for the rough months to come."

"It must have been very difficult for you."

"It was at first. But like all things, I grew accustomed to the darkness. I looked for the light in other things—and other people."

That made him think of Mariah. Under her mask of ire she was all light, all heat, fire and female. "I must return for Mariah." He stood, then paused. "Perhaps we can talk another time."

She sipped her lemonade. "I will see if my schedule—"

"We must talk, Tara."

She did not answer him. Her lips thinned and she placed her glass on the table with a little too much force. "I know why you've come."

"Do you?"

"Yes. Jane. She's a good girl, Zayad. She doesn't need to know the truth. Not now. Not yet. She doesn't need this kind of attention paid to her."

"I understand the wish for anonymity, believe me. But the truth remains—Jane is a princess." And whether her mother agreed with him or not, Jane deserved to know of her birthright.

A blanket of anguish seemed to encompass Tara as she thought about what he had said. Finally she gave him a nod. "Come back on Friday, then."

"I will be here."

"And you will not deny a semiaged woman her chance to explain?"

"Of course not."

An explanation, a true and full story, was the last thing—and the first thing—he wanted. He asked her to excuse him, then left the table to catch his breath and to help Mariah.

Seven

As they drove along the 101 freeway toward home, Mariah kept stealing glances at Zayad. Though he remained gorgeous and sexier than silk, he was also as stiff as a poker and incredibly pensive. She wondered at his mood, wanted to know if something had happened at Tara's, if the woman had said something to him while Mariah had been in the bathroom. But what? What would make him so rigid and thoughtful?

Her heart dropped a foot. She sure hoped it wasn't something about matchmaking. A quick setup was right up Tara's alley.

"Get the girl back on the horse" was her motto.

"A good ride will wipe that frown off your face, Mariah."

Ugh.

Maybe Mariah needed to set Zayad's mind at ease about her intentions to procure a date or a wild night of sex. "Say, Zayad, why don't you take the night off tonight?"

A semitruck passed them on the left, and he waited a moment before saying, "Pardon me?"

"Take a night off. From your 'duties.'"

"My duties?" He glanced over at her. "Do you mean *you?*"

"Yes. See, the thing is, I'm really jonesing for a pizza, and that's easy enough to order and have delivered. I'll make a place for myself on the couch, watch some TV—maybe an old black-and-white movie—and if I'm really feeling adventurous, dip into my work. Something tells me you need to get back to your work, too."

He sniffed almost regally. "There is plenty of time for my work."

"But isn't that little house you rented in the backyard calling you? I'm assuming it's an office space?"

"How did you know about that?"

"I've coveted that place for as long as I've lived here. I actually thought I might make it *my* office."

"What happened?"

"It's not in my budget."

"Ah."

"Anyway, the point is you've done enough for me." *And to me,* she mused, her skin warming at the memory of his arms around her and his mouth on hers. "Take some time for yourself."

His brow lifted. "Are you trying to get rid of me, Mariah?"

Just trying to keep myself a born-again virgin.

No.

Just trying to save myself the embarrassment of your rejection when I fling myself at you—and totally sober this time.

"Zayad, the truth is that you deserve a break. You've been amazing looking after me, making me meals, driving me to see Tara."

"I appreciate the thought, but I feel responsible for you and your well-being now."

"That's very gallant, but the knight-in-shining-armor routine is…" *Well, actually, it's so great I want to melt.*

"My mind will not be changed."

"But—"

"Like you, Mariah, I am a highly skilled debater."

"Yeah, I see that." She smiled.

He shifted into fourth gear, then third as he came off the highway and onto the main drag. When he turned onto their street, he asked, "Do you know much about swords?"

"Not much. But I find antiques and artwork very interesting." Actually she found it so interesting that she'd looked on the Internet this morning when Zayad had gone over to his apartment to change his clothes.

He pulled into the driveway with just a little too much speed, brought the SUV to a halt, then flicked off the ignition. "If you would like, we could share our worlds for the evening."

Fingers gripping the door handle, Mariah turned. "What do you mean?"

"You will come to my home for the pizza and, if it

amuses you—if you are truly interested—you could see some of my collection."

Her insides went tingly and raw. Weekend nights for old-maid Mariah Kennedy usually consisted of frozen food or takeout—because Jane was working—and a movie, just as she'd said she was going to do earlier. But this—this addition of a sexy man showing her his passion for antique weaponry… Well, strange as it may seem, that just couldn't sound any more fabulous.

But she smiled with only mild enthusiasm. After all, he didn't need to know how interested she was. "Maybe I could give you a fresh opinion on the pieces? Which ones you should sell and to whom? That kind of thing?"

A flash of humor crossed his face. "We will see."

Oh, he was so arrogant.

He got out of the car, came around to her side and helped her out. For a second he stood there, easing her arm about his shoulders, placing his hand unnecessarily on her hip. "We will see where the night takes us, yes?"

Heat snaked through Mariah and she found herself nodding as he lifted her into his arms.

"The man's name is Charles Waydon."

Thirty minutes later Zayad stood in his sparsely furnished living room, surrounded by yellow shag carpeting and badly stuccoed walls, and gave one of his most trusted aides the address of Mariah's client's unscrupulous husband. "He is to be watched twenty-four hours a day. I want to know where he goes, who he sees. I want photographs, Fandal. Even his refuse should be checked."

"Yes, sir."

"This is very important."

"I understand, sir."

Zayad turned his back on the man, snatched up the phone book. He would serve Mariah this pizza himself, order it himself. And he would not question his motives for wanting to perform such an inane act, for wanting to be just an ordinary man for tonight and for the next two weeks.

Though his servant might.

"If I may ask, Your Royal—sir?"

"Yes, Fandal?"

"Why are you helping this woman?"

"I have given her my word."

"Yes, but why? She is not the woman you seek."

No, she was not. But she was intriguing and beautiful and angry at the world. Her fire made him want to stay close, even though the warmth was not a sweet one. Her need for more than physical help intrigued him, made him want to give. Yes, he was used to handing out monetary assistance, but never had a woman wanted his friendship, needed his kindness of spirit.

It was somehow addicting.

But he could not allow his aide to know this. "She is the key to what I want. She is my sister's closest confidante. I am convinced that to know her is to know Jane." Zayad flipped through the Yellow Pages, looking for a pizzeria that sounded remotely distinctive. "Mariah Kennedy must be appeased, must be given all that she requires."

"I understand, sir."

"You may go, Fandal."

The man bowed and left the room.

Zayad grabbed his cell phone. What he did not understand was the intensity of his attraction to Mariah. His sympathy, yes. But gut-wrenching need?

In Emand when a woman caught his interest, he would offer her a night of pleasure, then anything she desired—anything but his heart. There had never been any mystery or deep ache of want with any of those women. Both he and his lover had always had their needs fulfilled and both had left content.

Mariah Kennedy was somehow different. With her caustic humor and the shadow of a deeply pained heart behind her eyes, Zayad felt he knew her. She had once said she did not believe in soul mates and he had concurred. If he was ever to believe in such a foolish notion, he might entertain the thought that this woman was his.

And he had only tasted her once.

His finger stabbed the keypad of his phone, dialing the number of Harrison's Pizza Shack. He could hold on to his desire for only a short time longer. If she were to kiss him again, he would not be stopped for something as irrelevant as honor.

He would have her.

"I'm a pepperoni kinda gal. Classic, a little spicy, but always satisfying." Booted foot propped up on a pillow, dressed in jeans and a black tank and bottom sunk into the same yellow shag that covered her own living room floor, Mariah grinned and slid a piece of the cheesy pizza into her mouth.

Across from her, leaning back against his tan couch,

Zayad ate his own slice of olive-and-mushroom. "Are you sure you are describing the pizza, Mariah?"

Mariah paused, ran the description back over in her head. "Sure, that could be me—but alas, only in the courtroom."

"Why is that?"

"In the courtroom I dress classically and am a pretty spicy litigator."

"And how are you satisfying?"

Now that is a question, Mariah thought, her pulse kicking. And asked with such a devilish twinkle in his eye, too. "Well, I hope in my victories."

"Of which there are many, I am sure."

Mariah took another bite of pizza, not wanting to correct his statement. In part because for the past year she'd rarely lost a case. Then, about a month ago, something had changed. Her attitude? Her drive? Something to do with confidence? She wasn't sure, but she'd lost her last three cases.

"What about you?" she asked, quickly deflecting.

"Me?"

"Yes, what kind of pizza are you?"

"I do not do well in describing myself."

"Well, give it a try. C'mon, we're being stupid and silly here—a rare thing for us both, I imagine."

He stared at her, grinned, and she wondered if he liked her quick, dry humor. Most men didn't seem to, or maybe they weren't sure how to respond.

"Green olives," he began thoughtfully. "Mushrooms and hot red pepper."

"Interesting. What's the description?"

"I have an acerbic nature, like the green olive.

Mushrooms tend to grow and mature in dark, remote places."

His expression looked pinched and he didn't elaborate on the mushroom thing. Something warned Mariah not to push him.

"And then there is the red pepper." He grinned, his eyes full of sin once again. "I, too, enjoy a little spice."

Thrill bubbled in Mariah's throat—the kind that comes from strange, arousing, nonspecific flirting.

It'd been a long time.

Zayad finished off his slice of pizza and the quarter of a beer left in his bottle. "I think it is time for my trip to the back house. If you would rather remain here and watch the television, I would not be offended. Looking over my work may be boring to anyone else but me."

Was he kidding? Three slices of pizza and a half-a-beer buzz. She was ready to see her sexy neighbor's swords and maybe even wrangle another kiss out of him. "No, I'd like to go."

"Very good." He stood. "The walk is not far but perhaps too much on your ankle—even with the support of your crutches. I will carry you, yes?"

She nodded and allowed him to lift her up once again. If truth be told, her ankle was feeling better, and using the crutches was easy and convenient. But Ms. Ultrafeminist was really starting to enjoy the comfort of this man's arms.

The cloudless night was generous with its stars, and the curve of moon shone brilliantly. Zayad carried her out the patio doors and onto the grass, wonderfully fragrant from just being cut that afternoon. The walk only took a few minutes, but the mood seemed to change with every step they took. From light to dim to deep in the backyard, very secluded and woodsy.

Mariah had always coveted the small gingerbread-like structure at the back of the property but had never seen inside it, as it always had been locked. Zayad pressed his code into the security keypad beside the door, and they entered. The first things Mariah saw were rough stone walls, beautiful hardwood floors and several hanging lights. A white couch and chair looked to have been pushed to one side of the room to make space for several large, black velvet boxes.

Zayad carried Mariah to the couch, making certain her ankle was elevated and that she was comfortable. Then he went to his cases and opened them. Metal gleamed up at him, and with great reverence he lifted two from the case and brought them to Mariah.

"These will soon be going to the two sons of Sheikh Jaran. He rules the country to the south of Emand."

"Wow, you've sold these to a sheikh?"

He only smiled as he placed the long sword on her lap. "This one is Persian." He ran his fingers slowly up the blade and over the intricately chiseled floral pattern.

Heat fused into Mariah's belly at the sight. If she asked, would he give her his attention, give her those glorious, sensual strokes that he was now bestowing on a sword?

"Notice the engravings," he said, his black eyes meeting hers. "In English it reads, 'Fear not my heart.'"

He slipped the sword from her lap and placed another in its place. This one had a lion-shaped hilt, and the blade was engraved with intricate latticework.

"You hold the Rajput sword. Very old and very rare." He leaned toward her and grinned. "It is said that Rajput marriages often took place between warring clans. Holding this sword, the groom sent a message to all who might take issue with the match that this woman was his and he would fight for her if the need arose."

Mariah gazed into his eyes, her pulse racing. "That's pretty dramatic."

"I would say so." His gaze flickered to her mouth. "But when a man and woman give themselves to each other, no person has the right to part them, do you not think so?"

Despite her issues regarding marriage, she found herself nodding. Who was she to disagree with such a romantic notion when Zayad sat so close, his eyes to hers, his mouth looking so warm and inviting?

She fairly sighed. Never in her life had she been so on edge, her skin prickly with heat.

"And this is how our young sheikh feels about his bride to be," Zayad said, breaking the spell just slightly. "I thought it an appropriate gift."

"An appropriate sale, you mean," Mariah corrected.

"Yes, of course." Outside the crickets started their song as Zayad stretched the Rajput sword out before her like a sacred offering. "Feel this."

She reached out, brushed her fingers over the metal. "Sharp."

"But beautiful, yes?"

Yes, he was. She wanted to kiss him so badly, she almost grabbed the blade and pitched it so she could grab him.

"I will put these away. I think we are done for tonight."

His words made her frown. Cleanup meant carrying her into the house and putting her and her ankle to bed—and not in a good way.

But she was wrong. After he put his swords away, he came to sit with her on the couch. "How is your ankle?"

"Heavy and a little achy." *Just like the rest of me.*

"Would you like to go inside?"

"Not just yet."

He nodded. "You must keep your ankle up until then and stay warm." He reached for a blanket and draped it over her. "Better?" he asked.

She didn't nod, couldn't nod. She didn't feel better. She felt uptight and needy and a little bit desperate.

He leaned in, brushed a strand of hair out of her eyes. "What is wrong? Is the pain very bad?"

He smelled of male and metal, and it had been so long. "Zayad, last night when we kissed…"

"Yes?"

He looked casually amused and she felt crazy embarrassed. But then again, she had started this, had blurted out phrases and words such as *last night* and *kissed*. There was no turning back. "Did you kiss me because you felt sorry for me?"

"What?"

"Was it because I was a little out of it?"

Why didn't she just ask him to pick her last for dodgeball? Or maybe—

But Mariah didn't get the chance to say anything more, think anything more. Zayad's hands went to her face, his mouth closed in and he kissed her so deeply, her heart fairly leaped out of her chest.

Then he eased back, his gaze fierce. "I do nothing out of pity."

"I just had to know if—"

"Do not say it again. You insult me."

He slid his hands down her arms to her waist. Sensation followed him, but Mariah couldn't revel in the pleasure. She didn't have time. He was under her shirt, his palm raking up her hot skin, cupping her breast. Heat penetrated the skin beneath her thin bra, and her nipple beaded instantly.

"Your hands feel like heaven," Mariah uttered, her breathing labored.

"And you are full of life, Mariah." His free hand held her neck as he nibbled her lower lip, then crushed her mouth beneath his again.

When he pulled back, Mariah released a breath.

"Wow," she said, her gaze as limp and desperate as her body.

"I do not know this word, but somehow it sounds appropriate."

"You *are* attracted to me," she muttered stupidly.

"What?"

"Nothing," she said, shaking her head.

Solemnity lit his eyes and he gripped her chin, held her steady. "Look at me, Mariah."

She lifted her gaze, feeling girlish and completely vulnerable.

"Do you not see the way I look at you?"

Did she? She didn't know. It had been way too long since she'd allowed herself to see a man for a man and not as the enemy in a courtroom. "I don't think I could notice such a thing now," she said a little sadly. "My past relationship really did a number on me and on my confidence as a woman."

"You were hurt?"

"Pretty badly."

He held her tightly against him. "And it still stings, yes?"

"Yes."

He said nothing for a moment, just looked at her. Mariah tried to decipher what was going on behind those black eyes, but he was a well-kept secret.

Finally he released her. "I do not wish to hurt you further."

"What do you mean?" she asked, suddenly feeling empty and cold, her breast aching for his touch again.

"I will not be another man who stings you."

"Wait. That's not what I meant by this. I…" Her words faded out, and she felt foolish. Because of what she'd said, there'd be no more kisses. No more caresses. An end to a delightful flirtation. And just when she was starting to come back to life.

"You are right to be cautious, Mariah," he began. "I am a man who cannot make commitments."

Her heart pitched, but she held steady. "I'm not asking for that."

"But you should. You deserve a good life with everything you desire. When you are ready to take such a chance again, of course."

Frustration bit at her, sexual and otherwise. "Listen, I don't need anyone to tell me what I deserve or don't deserve. Believe me, I've spent enough hours on the subject to write a self-help book. I want this—fun, sex, feeling lighter than air for the first time in a long time— with no strings."

He looked unsure and unconvinced. "I think it is time for our night to end, yes?"

No! she wanted to yell at him. But she didn't speak up, and he took control. He lifted her and carried her to the house, to her room and to her bed. She fell asleep fifteen minutes later, alone and dreaming of swords and a beautiful, frustrating man atop her nothing wearing but a devilish smile.

Eight

"I am very proud of you, Redet."

"Thank you, Father."

It was close to seven in the morning in California, and Zayad had arisen early from his restless sleep on Mariah's ridiculously small sofa in hopes of speaking to his boy. Zayad missed the child and wanted to hear his voice, hear that he was well and tell him that he would see him soon.

Leaning back in one of the deck's patio chairs, gazing out at an amazing sunrise, Zayad warmed with care for his son. "I wish I had been as intelligent as you when I was in school."

"You were not?"

Redet sounded very surprised and Zayad chuckled. "No. I had no head for figures or for the sciences, although I did fairly well in history."

"What of sport?"

"My father—your grandfather—would only allow me sport if I did well on my exams."

"And what sport would you have chosen if your grades had permitted?" Redet fairly giggled, for of course he knew.

Zayad smiled. "The sword, my son."

In the background Zayad heard a bell ringing and the scuffle of what he assumed were children milling about between classes.

"I must go, Father. My second class is to begin."

Zayad's heart clenched. He was a man and yet this boy made him ache like a woman. "I love you, my son."

"And you, Father. When will I see you?"

"In just a few weeks. I come to you straight from America and we will ride together and—"

"Have swordplay?"

"I have found a special sword for you. I will bring it with me."

From the open patio door Mariah listened. Granted, she'd heard just one side of the conversation, but she couldn't help but feel that one side was all she needed to hear.

Damn Zayad Fandal!

Why couldn't he be like all the rest of the charming, intelligent, handsome megalomaniacs she knew? Why did he have to be different—why did he have to have the whole package? Sure, he was a tad arrogant. But strangely that attitude was tempered with a caring, loving and generous spirit.

She watched him as he played with his coffee cup, his thumb gently circling the rim. Her belly tingled. His fingers were so long and tapered, so warm and so strong. She wished his hands would move over her again.

Fat chance, she told herself. Zayad had made his position pretty apparent last night. Mr. Noble was staying clear of her to protect her bruised and battered heart— a heart that had once been so overgrown with weeds, she'd thought she'd never escape its captivity.

But she had. Somewhat. And this man had swung the ax.

"May you remain safe and protected, my ami," Zayad said. Then he paused for a moment, and finally added, "Goodbye, Redet."

As he clicked off the phone, Mariah made a swift turn back into the house, but with her ankle she wasn't fast enough to avoid Zayad's gaze.

"Good morning, Mariah."

"Morning." She gave him a sheepish grin. "Sorry for eavesdropping."

"It is fine. You are walking on your ankle." His gaze swept her bare legs only partly covered with an oversize T-shirt. "Does it still pain you?"

"Only a little now. The boot keeps it pretty steady. I'm actually feeling pretty good today."

"How did you sleep?"

"Fine." *If tossing and turning while dreaming of you beside me is fine.*

"And what are your plans for today?"

"I have a lot of work to do."

"Well, sit down and have some breakfast first."

"Breakfast?" She saw nothing on the round mosaic table but his coffee cup.

"I will make eggs," he announced and stood, walked to her. "I am getting very good at eggs."

He looked like all the breakfast she needed, with his wet hair and black sweats, and she fought the urge to fake a pain in her ankle and fall. Maybe he'd lift her into his arms again, hold her close, his eyes penetrating hers as he said, "Let us go to bed…."

The shrill ringing of the telephone interrupted her idiotic fantasy and she turned to tug the receiver from the base on the wall.

"Hello?"

"Hey, it's me."

She glanced up at Zayad. "Hi, Jane, how's the teaching coming along?"

Zayad looked mildly interested, but didn't stay around to listen to her conversation. Instead he went to the kitchen and started on the eggs. Mariah went outside and sat in the chair he'd just occupied.

"I have the funniest story to tell you," Jane began with a devilish chuckle.

"Good. I could use a funny story right now."

After a night of sensual dreams and an early morning rise that consisted of only more thoughts of Zayad and his magical mouth, she needed something.

Jane laughed again, already three paces into her story about her student actress and a disastrous puff-pastry incident. "I warned her not to try it by herself, especially after a night of full-on partying, but you know, she's got a mind of her own. Needless to say, the fire department was called."

"Sounds great."

"Sounds great? What kind of medication are you

on? I just said—" Jane stopped short, sniffed. "Wait a minute. Where's Mr. Tall, Dark and Foreign right now?"

"Making breakfast," Mariah said sheepishly.

"Ohmigod, you slept with him."

"I did not."

"And he was supposed to be mine," she said dramatically.

"Oh, Jane. No. It's not—there's not—"

"Hon, I'm kidding. I never wanted the guy in the first place. I don't even know him or how gorgeous he is." She laughed. "C'mon, you so obviously have a crush. And that's wonderful."

"No, I do not have a crush," Mariah said sullenly as she picked up Zayad's coffee cup.

"Let yourself have a good time for once, Mariah. It's not going to kill you."

"How do you know?"

"You're such a cynic."

"Sad but true."

"Well, it's getting old and so are you."

"That not only rhymes, but it's a terrible thing to say."

"I'm not going to say I'm sorry," Jane said. "You're my best friend and I want you to be happy for once. I want you to go for it—for once."

Mariah mentally shook her head. How could she tell Jane that she was willing and able, but the man in question had integrity issues? "I'd better go. My eggs are getting cold."

Jane snorted. "Oh, sister, so are mine. We'd both better get going."

Mariah laughed and said goodbye to Jane. As she

hung up, Zayad walked through the patio door with two steaming plates of eggs.

"How is your friend?"

"She's good. A little irritated by her student, but otherwise good."

He didn't ask her why Jane was irritated, but asked instead, "Is she an impatient person?"

"Not at all."

"Perhaps she does not appreciate having to teach her skills to others?"

"No way. Last summer she spent an entire month teaching kids how to cook down at the community center." Why did she feel as though she were defending her friend? And why did Zayad make her feel as though she had to?

Mariah quickly finished off the last bite of her eggs. "Well, thanks for the breakfast, but I'd better get going on my work."

"Work?"

"I have a case to win, remember?"

"Ah. Yes." He wiped his mouth, tossed the napkin on his empty plate. "Did I tell you that I have a friend looking into this Charles Waydon."

Shock tore through her. "You do?"

"I said I would help you."

Yes, but she'd been thinking along the lines of brainstorming or something, not asking someone to do reconnaissance. She didn't get this guy. Didn't get him at all. Smart, sexy, helping her, taking care of her. What was he after? If he wasn't interested in Jane, why was he doing all this? Mariah took a deep breath. Could it even be possible that he liked her—really liked her—

but was a little freaked by his feelings and wanted to take things slow?

Oh, who was she kidding? What guy ever wanted to take things slow? "You did say you'd help me, but I didn't think—"

"You did not think I would follow through with my word?"

"No. Not in such an in-depth way."

He clucked his tongue. "Such cynicism, Miss Kennedy."

Her heart lurched. First Jane and now Zayad. She hadn't really listened to herself in the past few years, but she knew they were probably right on the money. She came across as cynical and very bitter. "The thing is, I don't expect you to help because you're honestly not obliged to—as in, you don't have to. If you want to stop right now, you're off the hook."

"I do not want to be off the hook."

Even biting her tongue couldn't stop her from asking. The question needed to be answered. "What is it you do want, Zayad?"

He leaned back in his chair, crossed his arms over his chest. "Let there be no work today. For either of us. I think you and I have seen too much work and not enough relaxation."

"I can't."

"You can. One day is not going to win or lose this case for you, but it actually might relax you enough to see your path better."

She sat up in her chair. "I can't afford to relax."

"When was the last time you were pampered, Mariah?"

NO POSTAGE
NECESSARY
IF MAILED
IN THE
UNITED STATES

BUSINESS REPLY MAIL
FIRST-CLASS MAIL   PERMIT NO. 717-003   BUFFALO, NY

POSTAGE WILL BE PAID BY ADDRESSEE

SILHOUETTE READER SERVICE
3010 WALDEN AVE
PO BOX 1867
BUFFALO NY 14240-9952

Get FREE BOOKS and a FREE GIFT when you play the...

LAS VEGAS GAME

Just scratch off the gold box with a coin. Then check below to see the gifts you get!

YES! I have scratched off the gold box. Please send me my **2 FREE BOOKS** and gift for which I qualify. I understand that I am under no obligation to purchase any books as explained on the back of this card.

▲ DETACH AND MAIL CARD TODAY! ▲

326 SDL D7Y5   225 SDL D7YV

FIRST NAME	LAST NAME

ADDRESS

APT.#	CITY

STATE/PROV.   ZIP/POSTAL CODE   (S-D-06/05)

7	7	7	Worth TWO FREE BOOKS plus a BONUS Mystery Gift!
🍒	🍒	🍒	Worth TWO FREE BOOKS!
🔔	🔔	♣	TRY AGAIN!

www.eHarlequin.com

Offer limited to one per household and not valid to current Silhouette Desire® subscribers. All orders subject to approval.

"Pampered? You're joking, right?"

"I am not."

She thought back, frowned, then thought back even further. "Well, senior year of high school I had an eyebrow wax before prom. 'Course, the woman made me look like something out of a *Star Trek* episode, so I don't think I'd call it pampering exactly."

He shook his head. "Pathetic."

"I would say so."

"Well." He stood up, reached for her hand and eased her to her feet. "I thought we would return to Ojai. They have a spa that is purported to be very good."

"A spa?"

"Saltwater baths are good for the ankle, and hotstone massages are simply…good."

Salt water and hot stones? It sounded exotic, sensual and wonderful—just like him. "I couldn't…."

"You will." He kept her hand in his, his thumb playing with her palm.

She swallowed hard. "And where will you be while I have stones and steam?"

"I will have a massage, as well. Perhaps we can experience a few of these treatments together, then have dinner?"

Mariah's heart beat wildly in her chest. Was it even possible that he'd changed his mind? That last night had been as tough on him as it had been on her? That he wanted to end the madness and just go for it?

He tipped her chin up. "Your mouth says little, but your eyes say yes."

"You're right, but…"

"But?"

"As wonderful as this sounds, it's too extravagant for both of us."

"I insist on taking you as my guest."

"No—"

"Yes. There will be no argument. I rarely participate in frivolity. I, like you, am committed to work. I wish to—what is this word you use?—spulge a little."

She laughed. "I think you mean *splurge*."

"Of course." His grin widened and he led her inside. "We will leave in one hour."

As Mariah readied herself for their day trip, Zayad finished up an important phone call. It had been short and to the point. Tara Hefner was expecting him at one o'clock today, and he would not be late.

A flash of guilt invaded his belly, but he pushed it aside. He had come to California for answers and he would have them.

Mariah gazed around the inn's sumptuous lobby and felt totally out of place in her jeans and white tank top. "Well if you wanted to *spulge* a little, this is how you do it."

"It is comfortable," Zayad said without enthusiasm.

Mariah snorted. "You must've really lived the high life before coming here, because this is way more than comfortable."

Grand in scale yet inviting and peaceful in its Mexican flavor, the Ojai Spa boasted beautiful yellow travertine tiles, overstuffed white couches, handmade rugs and a ton of exotic plants. She'd never seen anything like it. Heck, the only place her ex-husband had ever taken her was the Yellow Duckling Bed-and-Breakfast in Buelton—which also happened to be the pea-soup capital of the world.

"Welcome to the Ojai Spa." A fresh-faced young man and an exquisitely fit woman in her fifties, both dressed in white, sidled up to them with two cups of lemon-and-cucumber-scented water. "Sir, I will take you to your changing area, and Delilah will take you, Ms. Kennedy."

"Well, I guess this is goodbye," Mariah joked, giving Zayad a broad smile.

"Not for long, mi'nâr."

"What does that mean?"

He only grinned, then walked away from her, leaving the fresh-faced kid to run after him toward the locker room. For a moment Mariah just watched. He, too, wore casual attire—linen pants and a white shirt—and looked completely at home in the fancy surroundings.

Gotta be the attitude, she thought.

"Please come with me, Ms. Kennedy." Delilah led Mariah down a marble hallway and through a door marked Ladies. Once inside she found herself blanketed in the spa atmosphere. As she sipped her water, she took in the marble everything—the hot tub, steam shower and dry sauna. It was pure loveliness, and she was glad Zayad had talked her into coming here.

Delilah found Mariah a locker, then handed her a soft, white robe and one matching slipper. "I suggest you take your ankle brace off and enjoy a nice soak in the whirlpool before your massage, Ms. Kennedy. It's scented with rosemary and mint and is very relaxing."

"Okay, thank you."

Delilah nodded, then gave her a very coy smile. "Enjoy your stay and the massage." She pointed to a door at the far end of the locker room. "That will take you to your room. It's number five."

Mariah wasn't even going to try and figure out the woman's strange smile. Mariah was in paradise and she was going to enjoy every moment.

After a quick shower, she settled into the steamy, hot and deliciously scented whirlpool. Thirty minutes noomed like only seconds when she got out and slipped on her robe. *Must be the way of the spa,* she mused as she headed into massage room number five.

The lights in the room were dim and soft, and relaxing music played. The scent of vanilla permeated her nostrils and she breathed it in, smiling. In the center stood the luxurious massage table laden with towels and a note.

Curious, Mariah picked it up and read.

Please get undressed. Lie facedown. And prepare to be pampered.

Mariah shrugged out of her robe without a thought. After all, who was she to question the experts? With a decadent smile she climbed onto the table, slipped under the sheet and blanket coverlet and rested her head on the soft open circle.

The music, candle and dim lights did their job. She was just starting to drift off when the door opened and her therapist entered. The woman said nothing, merely folded down the blanket covering Mariah's back and got to work.

With one almost sensual stroke from her shoulders down to her lower back, Mariah came fully awake.

These were not feminine hands that massaged her—unless the woman had worked on a fisherman's boat for the past ten years. No, these were male hands, rough and strong.

She tried not to be prudish. After all, didn't people get massages from both sexes all the time? And she hadn't specified a preference at the front desk.

Maybe she should have.

Maybe this was why Delilah had been practically sniggering.

"Are you comfortable, Ms. Kennedy?"

Or maybe not.

Mariah's skin tightened, and all relaxation fell away. She lifted up and whirled around, the sheet covering her buttocks falling to one side. Standing above her in black drawstring pants, black T-shirt and magnetic black eyes was none other than Zayad.

He lifted a brow. "Too rough?"

Nine

She looked shocked and a little bit panicked, and Zayad wanted to put her mind at ease.

Along with several other areas on her beautiful body.

Acting the professional, he righted the loose sheet—though it pained him to do so, as her sweet backside was pure pleasure to behold. But he would start slowly, let her grow accustomed to his touch, ease her into relaxation.

He turned to a nearby table and applied some fragrant oil to his hands. "I apologize for startling you."

"What are you doing in here?"

"I thought perhaps you would feel more comfortable if I gave you a massage instead of a stranger."

In actuality he had been thinking about this all morning. He had nearly missed the exit for Ojai as the plan unfolded in his head. Mariah nude, her skin glowing with oils as he stroked her. Upon his arrival the spa had informed him that such a plan was out of the question, but as always, money had changed their minds. And it was a good thing, too, as there had been no female masseuses available today, and although Zayad hated to admit it, he did not want another man's hands on her.

"Instead of a stranger?" Mariah said with a stilted chuckle. "*You're* practically a stranger, Zayad."

He picked up her uninjured foot. "This is untrue. Have we not touched?" He began to knead her skin. "Have I not covered your mouth with mine? Is this the act of a stranger?"

Mariah felt as though she would melt right there. He did have a point. "No, not the act of a stranger."

He grinned, worked each toe with gentle yet firm strokes. "If I do not please you, tell me now and I will summon Larz."

"Larz?" Mariah laughed softly.

"One of the masseurs on duty. A large Swede with wild eyes."

"Is that so?"

"Yes." Zayad shook his head. "What a man like that could know about hot stone massage is nothing."

"And you do?"

"A common practice in my country." He took a stone from a small basket, held it up. "Shall I continue?"

"This is the strangest thing that's ever happened to me, but—"

"Yes?"

"All right." She turned, let her head fall back into the doughnut-hole thingy and let human nature take its course. "So, why did we have to come all the way here if you're such an expert?"

After a moment he said, "This massage is just one of many treatments—and the only one I will administer."

"No sugar rubs or deep-sea exfoliation back home?"

"No." He placed several stones on her back, then applied light pressure. "A woman's skin would not be fed sugar strictly for the purpose of beauty."

Heat fused into Mariah's belly, then quickly spread downward, between her thighs. "I'm almost too afraid to ask…"

"We use such things as…I think you call it foreplay."

"Foreplay?"

"It is not a common practice but a sensual game." He removed the stones, then massaged deep and wonderfully hard in the hot spots.

"A game," Mariah mumbled, feeling too good.

"Stimulating the skin for the woman while stimulating the tongue for the man."

Mariah fairly jumped with tension as his words hit her full force. Her mind took hold of an image and clung to it. An image she'd not allowed herself in years. A man's head between her thighs—this man's head between her thighs.

She inhaled deeply as her breasts tingled and her belly clenched.

And then hot stones were placed on the back of her neck and the soles of her feet.

She gave a startled gasp, or maybe it was a moan of pleasure—who could tell at this moment? She was hardly thinking straight.

"The heat will ebb," he told her soothingly. "Then fuse into your muscles."

As he spoke, the words he uttered turned to fact and she felt herself fall deeply into relaxation.

She let her mind drift, let her body go limp as he placed stones on her calves and her thighs. She didn't argue or feel embarrassed as he eased the towel from her and placed two hot stones on her bottom.

"How did you do it?" she asked, her voice as slow as her mind.

"Do what, Mariah?"

"This. This massage. The spa management would probably kick us out if they—"

"I have taken care of everything. There is no problem. Do not think of it."

"My mind should be a blank canvas, right?"

He chuckled. "No, you should be thinking of pleasure."

As if she could think of anything else at this moment. Well, besides Zayad on top of her, spreading her legs, entering her slowly as he nipped and kissed the back of her neck and the lobes of her ears.

"Please turn over."

Too lost in her fantasy, she muttered a raspy, "What?"

"Turn onto your back, Mariah."

"My back?"

"Yes."

The fantasy subsided and reality took over. Turning over meant she would be totally exposed—head to toe and everything in between.

The slow, rhythmic beats of her heart suddenly jumped and pounded. "Where's the towel?"

"You do not need it."

"I think I do."

She felt his face close to hers, his lips at her ear and his hands on her waist. "You have a beautiful body. Nothing to be ashamed of. If you could feel what simply looking at you has done to me, you would not fret as you do."

She turned her head, reveled for a moment in the feeling of his slightly stubbled jaw in that sensitive crevice between shoulder and ear. "Maybe I would like to feel what I have done to you, Zayad."

Maybe I desperately need to feel what I've done.

Maybe the thimbleful of self-regard I have left needs to feel it, too.

She felt him smile against her skin as he took her hand. "As you wish."

His lips remained by her ear while he put her hand on him. She took in a breath, felt suddenly dizzy. She'd never felt anything like him in her life. Rock-hard and very large. She wanted nothing more than to explore him, but Zayad didn't give her the time or the access.

He backed away. "Will you turn now?"

She slowly rolled to her back, trying to hide her satisfied smile. But it wasn't easy as his gaze moved over her, every hill, every valley.

His jaw looked tight with tension when he finally resumed his ministrations, taking her feet in his hands. "You would make a dead man come alive again, Mariah. And perhaps you already have."

His words tore into her, straight through her and into her heart. She suspected that this man was rarely vulnerable, rarely made such telling statements.

Up he moved to her calves, kneading the flesh with great care. Then to her knees and her quads. She felt so good, so on edge, so desirable. The closer his hands inched toward the pale curls at the apex of her thighs, the more her insides quaked with desperation, the more she imagined his fingers exploring and the steely hardness she'd felt a moment ago sliding slowly into her body.

He placed more stones on her hip bones, making her suck air through her teeth, sending heat to her core.

He placed warm stones at her breastbone and rib cage, arousing her belly, causing her breasts to tighten, her nipples to bead.

Her breath caught in her chest, then followed quick and slightly labored. She looked up, found him watching her, his nostrils flared, his lips thin.

"Do you enjoy?" he asked.

"Yes. Very much." *What a hell of an understatement.*

She wondered what he would do next. Remove the stones and finish the massage, then turn off the music and call it a day—leave her in a state of sexual panic and frustration?

But he didn't massage and he didn't leave. He leaned down and kissed her mouth. There was nothing soft or gentle about it. And she was glad. She wrapped her arms around his neck, pulled him on top of her, moaned as she felt the delicious weight of him.

He pressed openmouthed kisses down her neck, her collarbone, removing stones as he went—lapping at her hot skin with his tongue. Then he boldly took one full breast into his mouth.

Mariah whimpered, maybe even cursed—she wasn't sure. Zayad's tongue whipped over her jutting nipple, then he took her between his teeth. Squirming on the table, Mariah held his head in her hands.

But not for long.

He moved down, kissing her belly, grazing his teeth over her warm hip bones. Breath coming quickly, Mariah came up on her elbows to see him, watch him as he kissed and laved and nibbled her aching skin.

Lower he moved, clear on his target. But the awkwardness of the massage table had him leaving her for a moment. He stood, scooped his hands under her bottom and eased her forward. Her knees now bent, he pressed her legs apart and grinned.

Anticipation threatened to overwhelm her as he lowered his head and captured her with this mouth. She nearly screamed and muffled the sound with her hands.

He suckled her, let his tongue dance up the bundle of nerves at her core.

It had been too long, far too long.

She let her head fall back.

Heat built inside her and she knew she would orgasm quickly. She hated the fact but didn't want him to slow, didn't want herself to slow.

She arched her hips, pumped against his mouth. Then she stopped, stilled. Heat and pressure and tension all conspired, led her over the moon and into deep pleasure.

Over and over the waves hit, and she bucked and arched and moaned. Until finally the ebb came and she started to breathe again.

"Mariah…"

She reached out for him, but he stayed where he was, even bent to pick up her towel.

With supreme gentleness he placed the cotton over her. "I must leave you now."

"No." She sounded like a child, but she didn't care. She'd only gotten half of what she wanted.

"I must." He bent over her, kissed her mouth. "I will see you in two hours, yes?"

She sighed, knew it wasn't wise to take more right here, right now. "All right."

He went to the door, turned back. "You had much pleasure?"

"Yes."

He nodded, then left, and Mariah sat up. She felt tight and happy and sad and unsure. She was no longer the bitter, chaste divorcée. She was now a woman on the verge of intense desire for a man she hardly knew and didn't trust.

He had hated to leave her.

Zayad pulled into the assisted-living-center parking lot, found a space and cut the engine. Even though a sign marked Guest was directly in front of him, he saw only a dimly lit room, a massage table with white towels and one of the most beautiful women he had ever seen lying naked atop them, bucking and gasping with climax.

He inhaled, tried to rid his mind of her—for now, at least. But it was impossible. Her scent lingered, as did the feeling of her skin on his palms.

Damn his lack of control. He had come here to question Tara, not to find himself fantasizing—and certainly not to find himself feeling actual need for a woman he would never see again after his two weeks were through.

He ripped his keys from the ignition and got out of the car, walked across the lawn to Tara's bungalow door. He would have to fight his desire for Mariah Kennedy. He could not allow this kind of pull, this kind of distraction, when he had work to do here.

After two decisive raps on the door, it opened and the lovely older woman who had so captivated his late father stood before him.

"Good afternoon, Zayad."

"Ms. Hefner."

"Tara, please." She smiled, stepped aside so he could enter.

"Thank you for letting me come, Tara. I know you did not have to."

"I'll admit I'm just as curious as you are." She showed him into the same living area where they had begun their last visit. She had some lemonade and cookies set out on the coffee table. She took a glass and started for the pitcher of lemonade.

"Allow me," he said.

"Thank you."

He poured her a glass, then eased it into her hand. He also took a cookie and placed it on a napkin in front of her on the table.

"Thank you," she said with a grin.

Her ability to sense or hear the smallest of movements amazed him. "If I may ask, how did you lose your eyesight?"

"I have macular degeneration."

"I am sorry."

"I'm not."

"Really?"

"Well, that's not entirely true. I would love to see my work, my child's face, Mariah in the courtroom and your wicked grin—the same as your father's, I'll bet. But I can't have those things. I see in a different way and I came to realize that sometimes that is a good thing. I believe now that it was a precious gift to have my sight taken from me." She paused, smiled. "You're shocked by that, right?"

He took a cookie. "I am intrigued."

"Good answer." She also reached for her cookie. "When I lost my sight, it was slow. Darkness took over the light little by little. Before, I had lived a life of judgments, as I think we all do. What we see on the outside is, of course, what is on the inside. We hardly question this. But when you start losing the ability to see the outside of anything, you're forced to deal only with the heart, with the deeds, with the real stuff."

She took a breath, then smiled. "All judgments left me, and instead I had questions. No more anger or cynicism or 'why mes,' only curiosity and compassion." She looked at him, her eyes so blue, so kind, yet there was a little sadness there. "I say no regrets, true. But I'll admit I've always had a hole in my heart for a time that ended too shortly."

The cookie felt dry in his mouth. "The three days with my father?"

"Yes." She leaned back in her chair. "He was an amazing man. Our time together was magical. Morally right or wrong, it was the best three days of my life—except for Jane's arrival."

"You loved him?"

"Very much."

Zayad's chest tightened. Why had he asked that? He did not care for love. This was about Jane and her future. This was about wanting to know why his father had given so much of himself to this woman. Who she was. Perhaps it was also about knowing his father better.

She nibbled on the cookie and tucked her feet up under her. "I know this is probably the last thing you want to hear, but it's part of the story. I thought your father cared for me a great deal. When he left, he told me he loved me. But we both understood that we belonged to different worlds. And of course, he had a family."

"Yes," said Zayad with mild tension.

"And I would never have messed with that. But I just couldn't believe that what we shared was all a lie. That he didn't care for me at all. And it kills me to know that he didn't even care for the life growing inside of me."

Though Zayad hadn't come to ease the pain of his father's mistress, he knew he must say something. "I am certain he would have cared for Jane if he had known."

"Known?" For the first time since he had met Tara, she looked completely unsettled. "Of course he'd known, he just didn't—"

"My father did not know of your pregnancy, Tara."

Her brows knit together. "What?"

"He knew nothing."

"No, that's not possible." She shook her head. "His aide said—"

"The man did not inform my father of your calls or

of Jane's existence. He felt he was protecting my father and the royal family from—"

"Don't say it." She put her hand in the air as though to block all negativity from reaching her. Then she let it fall, and her face fell along with it. "Are you really telling me the truth? He never knew he had a daughter?"

"He did not."

"So, he didn't lie to me." It wasn't a question. A look of hope crossed her features, and she took a moment to just breathe. Then suddenly she looked pensive again. "Why have you come to America, Zayad? Why have you sought out Jane? To tell her about her heritage or to see if she's worthy enough to accept it?"

"Both."

She nodded, her lips thin. "You will not hurt my child."

"I have no intention of hurting her."

"She's innocent. I never wanted to burden her with stories of her father. She knows nothing of this."

"She must."

Tara paused, bit her lip, shook her head. "Yes. I suppose so."

"I want to talk with her when she returns from Los Angeles."

"No, I will tell her when she comes to me next week." She nibbled more on her cookie. "As much as it pains me, we all have to know our truths."

Zayad nodded, agreeing fully. Truth could be a bitter pill to swallow, but there was no way to escape it.

"And what of my other child?" Tara said.

Zayad's brows drew together. "Mariah?"

An almost sad smile hovered about her lips. "She's

growing fond of you. She hasn't looked twice at a man in ages. To be honest, it scares me to death."

"She has nothing to fear from me."

"You're going back to Emand, right? To your work and your life."

"Yes."

"And you're going to leave her here broken-hearted. I've been there, Zayad. In love and alone. It's not something I wish for Mariah."

"Mariah does not have such feeling for me."

"Maybe not right now but soon. I see it in her."

"You see—"

She smiled. "I sense it. Please be careful. With both of my girls, okay?"

"I will."

When Zayad pulled away from the center, he felt as confused as ever. He had wanted to hate this woman, to tell her that his father could not possibly have loved her, to laugh at her story and admissions of care for the sultan. But he could not and did not, as those were the reactions of an affronted child.

He took each curve of hill a little too dangerously. He was beginning to feel something new—an out-of-control feeling that worried him. He wished he could speak of his fears with Mariah. He did not know why, but he felt close to her, a friendship as well as desire. But it was unwise to engage her in emotion. If what Tara had said was true, he could only allow himself the closeness of skin and sweat and desire.

A shot of disappointment went through him, and he despised himself for feeling so. When had this soft side where women were concerned overtaken him?

The ocean came into view.

He knew exactly when. It had been early evening several days ago, and a frustrated but heavenly lawyer had run headfirst into his chest.

He had surprised her.

Mariah had been under the impression that after several awesome spa treatments they'd be heading back home. But no. After her last treatment, a wonderful woman had come for her, led her out of the spa building and into the hotel portion of the inn. With just a sentence or two of explanation she'd left Mariah in the most gorgeous of suites overlooking a small lake littered with ducks.

Zayad had arranged this, the woman had told her. He wished for Mariah to relax and he would be here in an hour for dinner.

Mariah wanted to feel shocked by his boldness and maybe muster up some pangs of anxiety about the whole thing, but she couldn't get herself to feel anything except excitement.

Well, that and a little frustration that she hadn't brought anything but the casual clothes she was wearing. She was going to have dinner in this magnificent suite overlooking a lovely lake during sunset and she had no fabulous outfit.

Of course, she didn't own all that many fabulous outfits to choose from. And what really went with a brown ankle boot?

But when she walked into the white bathroom, she saw that Zayad had further surprises in store. Her toiletries were set up on the counter, and the two prettiest dresses she owned hung on the shower rod, along with one she didn't recognize. It was a pale yellow silk slip dress, very beautiful and very expensive looking.

Without a thought she knew Zayad had bought it for her and she also knew she was going to wear it tonight.

After a quick shower, a long blow-dry and some light makeup application, she let the chef in, then reclined on the couch and waited for her date to arrive. As she sat there, her senses being pummeled by the scents of roasted lamb and fresh rosemary bread, she thought about the afternoon and specifically about the massage table. Shivers of desire rippled through her, but there were far more nerve-racking sensations to contend with. For the first time in years she'd allowed a man to touch her both emotionally and physically.

She was opening herself to getting hurt again.

Maybe if she didn't view this affair as she had her marriage, she could cast aside her fears about getting hurt. There is no commitment here, no words of love spoken, no promises made. She didn't have to have expectations of him, only pleasure for however long it lasted.

As the door opened and Zayad walked in, she wondered if that were possible.

Looking unbelievably handsome in a black suit and a crisp white shirt open at the collar, Zayad stopped in front of her. "You look beautiful, Mariah. The color of the sun is magnificent on you."

"Thank you, and thanks for the dress."

"It is nothing."

It was more than he could ever know. No man had ever bought her anything so personal.

"How was the rest of your day?" he asked.

"Wonderful."

"And your ankle?"

She lifted her booted foot so he could see. "Much better."

His gaze moved over her bare skin, from toes to midthigh. "Are you hungry?"

You have no idea. "I could eat."

"Our chef comes highly recommended." He helped her to her feet and led her over to the preset table in front of the French doors. "Can I pour you some wine?"

"That would be great, thanks."

The chef came out and placed the chicken, bread and salad between the white candles and red roses, then nodded at Zayad and left the suite.

When a curious Mariah turned to Zayad, he smiled. "I thought it best if we could dine alone. Is this all right?"

Alone with Zayad…

She smiled as much to herself as to him. "Of course." She took a sip of the white wine, then asked, "So, what did you do today while I was getting pampered?"

He offered her some bread. "I had some business to attend to. One of which was planning our dinner."

"Well, you did a great job. It's beautiful." *And you're beautiful.* She looked up at him. *And I don't know if I can pretend this means nothing more to me than sex.* "Everything's perfect."

Wineglass to his lips, he studied her. "Something is wrong."

"No."

His gaze bored into her. "Are you having regrets?"

"About what?" As if she didn't know.

"Allowing me to be your masseur instead of the Swede?" He reached across the table and took her hand. "For, you understand, I could not abide him touching you."

Delicious shivers crawled up her spine. "Why?"

"I would not like it."

She forced herself not to ask why again. "I don't think I would've liked it much, either."

"Then I was wrong? You have no regrets?"

She shook her head.

He played with her fingers. "There is something I must tell you, Mariah."

Oh, God, what? You're a woman? You have a woman? You want to bring a woman into our bed tonight?

She was going completely nuts.

He released a weighty breath. "I am only in California for a short time."

Not icky, not perverted, but definitely not good. "Okay."

"I want to be…as honest as I can with you."

"I appreciate that." *Sort of.*

"You see, my life is in Emand, my work, my son and—"

"Zayad, I understand. Really." She didn't want to hear any more. She knew now that this affair would end. Heart strings really wouldn't be attached. Knowing that, she simply could enjoy herself with no worries about the future. His honesty, though heartbreakingly disappointing, was refreshing. For once a man wasn't lying to her. She gave him a soft smile. "Let's talk about something else, okay?"

He took her hand and kissed it, then released her and reached for his wine. "What other treatments did you have, and were they as good as your massage?"

Flirting. Yes, this she could do, this she wanted. "The body exfoliation was pretty good."

"This is the one with sugar, yes?"

"Yep."

"To make the skin softer?"

Mariah laughed. "I hope so."

"I would be willing to judge this, if you would like."

"You'd be willing, huh?"

He flashed her a devilish grin, stood up and walked around behind her. He put his hands on her shoulders, let his palms rake down her arms. "Yes. Very soft."

She sighed, closed her eyes.

"But I feel I must explore further to make certain."

His hand slipped inside her dress. Her breath hitched as he palmed her bare breast, as he let his thumb move back and forth over her swollen nipple.

She released a moan. Forget food, forget talking and flirting and getting to know each other more. They had waited long enough, hadn't they? She needed this. Her body needed this. Clearly he did, too.

She stood, turned and faced him. "Take me to bed."

She waited for him to say no, not yet, after dinner. But he didn't. His eyes were black as ink and hot as hell as he nodded and said, "Yes?"

"Yes." She smiled, knew she looked desperate, on fire, totally ready and willing.

Zayad lifted her up, and she buried her head in his neck.

Ten

Mariah closed her eyes as Zayad laid her gently on the bed. She'd wanted this moment to happen, fantasized about it day and night, hoped against hope that Zayad was as into her as she was into him. But now that it was happening, she couldn't help but feel a bit self-conscious. After all, her last relationship had ended over sex. True, it had been her husband and another woman who had actually had the sex, but she'd always wondered if she'd driven him into that woman's arms—if she was a horrible lover.

But all thought died as Zayad lowered himself on top of her and claimed her mouth. The weight of him made her high, his chest smashed against her breasts, his erection pressed gloriously against her belly, the way he rubbed his lips back and forth over hers, swiped her upper lip with his tongue.

Mariah groaned with approval and arched her hips to meet him, her underwear feeling wet and confining. Her hands went around his neck, plunged into his hair.

"You want this, yes?" he uttered, tense.

"I want you," she answered breathlessly.

Zayad tugged at the thin straps at her shoulders, then pulled her dress down. She wore no bra, and he looked ready to feast. With one hand he explored the fullness of her breast, his thumb and forefinger torturing her stiff nipple. With the other he snuck under her dress, over her panties, and palmed the swollen V between her thighs.

"You feel too good, Mariah." He stroked her, quickly and lightly, then eased two fingers inside of her.

Her breath caught in her throat and her body quivered with the need to release. But she held on. She wanted to have him inside of her as she climaxed this time.

Zayad must have sensed her urgency or he simply couldn't wait. In seconds he had her dress off and his own clothing removed. And in mere moments his hands returned to her hot skin and his mouth found her nipple.

Heat pooled in her belly, and her hands raked down his broad back, down to his buttocks. She dug her fingers into his taut flesh, pressed him hard and rough against her. Desperation filled her. "Please, Zayad. I can't wait. I don't want to wait."

He lifted off her, reached over to the side table. With deft fingers he quickly protected her. "I am without control tonight. Forgive me."

She didn't understand him but didn't have time to ask as he rose up and positioned himself over her.

Her breath coming in gasps, Mariah spread her legs

wide. She was tight and he was large, but as he inched his way to paradise, she felt an all-consuming pleasure.

And then he was through and deep, and her breath caught in her throat.

He fit her perfectly.

Maybe this was different. Maybe this was the something real she'd never thought existed.

His eyes probed her soul as he dipped his head and kissed her hungrily. When he eased back from her mouth, he remained deep inside her, but his hand disappeared behind her head. He brought back a pillow, then easily slipped it under her hips without breaking their connection.

"What is this?" she asked.

"It will make your experience more fulfilling."

"I don't think that's possible."

His smile was soft, but his eyes were filled with intensity and heat. A heat she understood, and wanted to express. She squirmed beneath him. He grinned, this time with wicked intent, and he rose out of her, then pushed back in. His strokes were long and liquid as his pulse jumped in his temple.

Tension built like a rising dam inside her, and she knew she was close. She wanted to curse, wanted to cry. She wanted to stop and start again. But it was no use. And when he reached under her hips, lifted her higher, his rhythm changing, quickening, rising to a frantic pace, she leaped, then fell—sank into the waves and the quakes of pleasure, the heat and all of the beautiful electric pulses.

Zayad ground his hips against hers and called out in a husky male growl as his body quivered and shook. It was an amazing sight.

He dipped his head and kissed her again, a salty, searing kiss that sent another shudder through her. Then he sat up, brought her with him so they were both sitting, facing each other. It was an incredibly intimate gesture, and Mariah felt so connected to this man, she wanted to bury her head in his chest. But he wouldn't let her. He clearly had something to say.

"You have much passion, Mariah. But it has been buried deep, yes?"

Her throat went tight. "Yes."

His hands found her face. "You must release it."

Mariah stilled, not sure of what he was telling her. Was she not passionate enough? Her gaze fell. She felt as if she'd failed again. No wonder her husband had gone with another woman. Maybe she was frigid or something. "Am I a horrible lover?"

"No." He chuckled, tilted her chin up so she was forced to look at him. "This is not what I mean. You are wonderful. You are a woman filled with heat, with deep thought and a touch so extraordinary it makes me hard as stone."

"But—"

"There is no but." Zayad kissed her. "Your body gave like no other. You were wild and wonderful. I want not just the pleasure but the hurt behind your eyes, as well. I must release it. I must make you release it."

"Why?"

His gaze flickered, and he looked pained suddenly. "I do not know."

"I really don't think it can be released, Zayad. Or maybe I just don't want to show it to anyone ever again." The intimacy growing a little too tough to handle, she tried to move away from him. But Zayad wasn't about to let her feel her fear alone, much less let her leave.

"Tell me about this man who has made you question everything and everyone."

She shook her head. She didn't talk about him, about what happened, to anyone. Especially not now.

"Tell me," Zayad insisted.

He held her tightly and carefully, but held her to him until she finally said something. "He was handsome and charming and a great businessman—and one helluva good liar."

"And why is he no longer your husband?"

"He didn't want me." Tears threatened and she wanted to kick herself. "He wanted another woman instead."

"He was a fool."

She looked down.

He pulled her to him and lay back down on the soft pillows. "We must pity him. For he made many mistakes and they cost him the most amazing woman in the world."

Mariah put her head to his chest, feeling emotional and confused. She took a deep breath. "No more of him. Tell me about your homeland. Make me think beautiful thoughts."

"All right." He kissed the top of her head. "Ah, Emand. Nowhere in the world is there a better place. Dawn is my time. I love it." He played with her hair as he spoke. "The sun is just making its entrance. So slowly, you feel as if you have wasted many hours in its presence. Yet you feel no regret for it. The sand of the desert is cool, a dirty brown color, before the sun meets it. Then it turns copper. The gardens are fragrant and lush, the mountains and lakes pure and untouched. The people, though deep in their traditions, are generous and forgiving."

"Why would you leave such a place? Even for a short time. It sounds like paradise."

He pulled her to him, held her tightly. "Business can take you away from even the most wondrous of settings."

Neither one of them spoke after that. They cuddled and stroked until sleep took them both. Mariah went willingly into her dreams. It was the first time in four years she'd slept next to a man.

It was the first time in Zayad's life that he had slept beside a woman.

He had always appreciated being alone. There was a certain comfort in it, an understanding between himself and his lover that what had transpired between them in bed would not transcend his desire for solitude.

Zayad stood at the balcony window of their suite, watched the black sky being eaten up by the dusk that came an hour or so before dawn.

Last night he had consciously pulled Mariah into his arms and fallen asleep. He had wanted to wake up with her, wanted to make love to her again, wanted her open in both mind and spirit beside him. He wanted to rid her heart and mind of that bastard she had called her husband.

He closed his eyes for a moment, then opened them hoping he would see gardens and beyond, miles and miles of sand. He missed Emand. He felt like a boy for feeling that way, but it could not be helped. After all, he was acting as a child—forgetting why he was here, what he was after, all for the sake of a beautiful and enticing woman.

He heard her get out of bed, heard the rustle of a sheet as she walked. She came to stand beside him and he glanced her way. The washed moonlight illuminated the thin white sheet wrapped around her from breast to foot. Her skin looked soft from sleep. Her blond hair fell about her shoulders. She didn't say anything, just moved in front of him and splayed her fingers on his chest. He released a breath, and she let her fingers snake downward, over his belly, to the black hair below his navel.

He was hard before she fisted him.

Her eyes on his, she massaged him, stroked him, made him groan with need, then when he was ready to take her, she released him. Slowly she lowered to her knees, thrust his legs apart. His gut tight with anticipation, Zayad gripped the top of the doorway. Mariah cupped his buttocks with one hand and eased him into her mouth with the other.

Zayad nearly howled.

She let her fingers dig into his backside as she suckled him deep. Then she drew back and flicked the tip of him with her tongue. Zayad reached behind himself and took her hand, squeezed. He knew it was a sweet, sentimental gesture, but he could not help it. It was how he wanted her.

She pumped him slowly and deeply, and when he felt himself on the brink of release, he uttered a hoarse, "Mariah," and eased her back and to her feet.

"We will find pleasure together, yes?" he said, his tone gruff.

Her lips wet, her eyes brilliant with desire, she pushed him back against the bed. Zayad grinned, for he knew she was casting aside her fears and taking control, taking what she wanted for the first time in a long time. But that smile quickly waned as she said, "Lift me up, put me on top of you."

His mind near to exploding, Zayad forgot to think and did as she instructed. "Wrap your legs around me."

"Yes."

They were clumsy, awkward, but it didn't matter. He was sheathed and inside of her in seconds, thrusting furiously as Mariah held on for the ride. Her head fell back and he devoured her neck, his teeth raking down, his tongue smoothing up.

And when he slipped his arm to her waist and she fell farther back, he took her nipple into his mouth, pushed her into release, then followed her, exploding into the predawn air.

"We have photographs, sir."

Sitting at a small glass table on the balcony of his suite, Zayad took a swallow of orange juice, then switched his cell phone to his other ear. "Are they worthy, Fandal?"

"Oh, yes, sir."

With a quick glance to the door, Zayad grinned. When Mariah returned, she would be very pleased indeed. On his insistence, she had gone down to the spa to have a manicure and pedicure before they left for home. She had fought him on it, she wanted to stay in bed, make love again. But Zayad had wanted to spoil her in more ways than sexual. If he had his way, they would fly to Los Angeles this very afternoon and he would take her to the finest shops in Beverly Hills— clothing, diamonds, anything she wished.

Many women he had known, including Redet's mother, would be vastly contented with such a plan, but something told him that Mariah would want nothing more than a lazy day in bed with him, holding him as he kissed her mouth, neck, breasts…. She had once had a man of means and had found it unfulfilling.

The thought made his chest tighten. He was growing contrite. He knew he must tell Mariah the truth—and soon.

"I would like to see one photograph," he told Fandal.

"I can bring it to you, sir. As you know, we are just two floors down."

He had almost forgotten. Almost. "No. Fax it to me immediately. Your best one."

"Of course, sir."

Zayad gave his aide the room's fax number, then hung up. He went inside and waited by the phone. In under a minute a photograph ambled through the fax. Zayad had it in his hands in seconds and looked it over thoroughly.

He grinned. His men had done well, and had laid four separate pictures on one sheet of paper. The top two were of the man and woman kissing outside a motel room. One of the bottom ones, though perhaps a bit too voyeuristic, was of the couple making love inside the room. And the last one was of the couple having dinner in a restaurant, very close. Zayad did not want to know how his photographer had gotten these, nor did he care.

Suddenly the door to the suite burst open and Mariah entered.

"The manicurist had some bad Chinese and had to go—" Mariah paused, stared at the paper in Zayad's hand. "What's that? Work?"

He shook his head, held out the fax to her. "I told you I would help you. I have a man tailing your client's ex-husband at all times. These are photographs of him and his lover."

Brow furrowed, Mariah made a beeline for the fax. She studied it hard from every angle, then looked up. "They're good—and you're amazing for going to all the trouble of helping me. Thank you."

"There is a but, yes?"

She nodded, dropped the fax on the table. "I'm afraid they won't help my case."

Eleven

"Why not?"

Mariah gave Zayad a bleak smile. "They only show that he's messing around now, not that he did before. Sure, it'll help, showing that he's lied about seeing someone recently. But it's his past infidelities—the affair he had while they were married—that's going to bring around the justice, show him as the liar he is."

"I see."

He was clearly disappointed, and the sight filled Mariah with gratification as much as empathy. Never in her life had a man cared this much about her and her pursuits. Zayad Fandal was a great lover and he was an amazing friend. She was lucky to know someone like him.

Though a little cursed, as well.

She went to him, put her arms around him. "You've been wonderful. Thank you."

"I have not found you your answers."

"You've done the best you could."

"No, but I will."

"I'll figure this out."

"With my further assistance."

She looked up at him, melted in the heat of his dark gaze. "You've done too much already—"

"I will see this through, Mariah."

"Why is it so important to you?"

"Because it is important to you."

Her heart squeezed just then, and she let her head fall against his chest. He felt so solid, so strong, his heart beating against her cheek. He made her feel like a woman, feminine and cared for, and she couldn't deny it any longer—she was in love with him.

Maybe these feelings in such a short time were crazy and stupid, but she didn't care. She felt alive. Bitterness had gotten her through the pain, but now it was stopping her from not only loving, but living.

A thought snaked into her brain. A thought built on hope. If Zayad had fallen in love with her, too, or was on his way, would he stay?

"There is another reason I wish to help you."

His words vibrated against her cheek, their content sending spirals of nerves through her belly. Was he about to tell her how he felt? What he wanted? Or was this an admission of something outside of them?

"I also do this for Redet."

Her belly clenched. "Your son." Of course. Of course he couldn't stay. He had a child in his country. A child he loved above all others. And if he even contemplated leaving his son to be with her, he'd be no better than the jerks she fought against in court.

Irony sucked.

There was no way this could work, she realized, her heart plummeting into her shoes. Her life was here, and his life was in Emand.

Zayad stroked her hair. "This man you battle, this man who cheats and lies on the woman he is bound to, does not deserve his child."

Anger and disgust filled his tone. Two emotions Mariah felt, as well. But she detected more than anger. There was a thread of disappointment, maybe even fear, in his voice. She didn't know his history, what he and his family had been through. She couldn't help but wonder if it played a part in those hidden threads of emotion. Or if what she was hearing was just his feelings regarding Redet and his mother.

She tilted her head, stared up at him. So handsome, so chiseled—such the look of the warrior about him. He made her weak with desire, yet his conviction and spirit made her admire him so much.

"Kiss me?" she said.

Fire lit his eyes, and he bent and covered her mouth with his own. All thought of anything but love evaporated into the gentle morning breeze floating in from the suite's French doors.

There were ten messages on the answering machine when they got home at noon, and Mariah knew she was in big trouble. All but three were from Jane.

There were several "This actress is making me insane

and I need to vent," a few "Where the hell are you?" and one "Call me back or I swear I'm going to call the police."

After changing her clothes and telling Zayad she'd see him later, Mariah picked up the phone. She paused before dialing, a little shocked at herself. She hadn't told Jane where she was going and what she was doing. She'd completely forgotten her soul sister, her mind totally focused on Zayad. After allowing a man to rule her thoughts and actions for many wasted years, she wasn't entirely sure how she felt about that.

"I could kill you right now," Jane barked, sounding far more relieved than angry.

Opting for a lighter mood, Mariah teased, "If only you weren't a hundred miles a way."

"Right." She took a breath. "So, how's the ankle?"

"Much better," Mariah said. "Listen, sis, I'm sorry I didn't tell you where I was going. It was just so spur-of-the-moment, ya know?"

"No, because you haven't done anything spur-of-the-moment in I don't know how long. Especially with a guy."

"This guy," she almost sighed, "as difficult as it is for me to admit, makes me forget my name, my responsibilities, my—"

"Mind?" Jane asked, her mild irritation morphing into an affectionate chuckle.

"Yes, actually."

"I can't believe you've fallen for our neighbor." Jane snorted. "It's so *Peyton Place*."

"He's not going to be our neighbor for very much longer."

"What do you mean? Where's he going?"

"Back to his country." The words felt like sandpaper on her tongue.

"What? He's leaving you after all this."

Mariah took a breath. For the four years that she and Jane had been roommates, she'd always thought that Jane was the one who had done the influencing—her great food, her positive attitude. Some of that stuff had actually rubbed off on Mariah—or the hope that it would have rubbed off, especially the cooking part. But the truth was, Mariah and her negative, supposedly realistic, views on life and love had rubbed off on Jane, and now she was spouting that fear-based crud back at Mariah.

Irony really did suck.

Mariah didn't want to be the poster girl for sad women anymore. She'd tasted love again, and even though it might not last, it was spicy and addicting and she wanted more, no matter what the consequences.

"Jane, the thing is, he has a son. He can't stay here because he wants to be close to him. You know how I feel about that."

Silence ate up a moment or two. "Sure. Jeez, of course I do. What about going with him?"

"He's never mentioned it, and I'm not going there."

"Why not?"

"I won't push him. That'll only make me look desperate and make him feel cornered."

"But maybe he needs—" Jane never finished her sentence as a shrill shout from the other end of the phone had her cursing.

"I gotta go, M," Jane said. "Cameron Reynolds calls. I'll see you in a couple of days, 'kay?"

"'Kay."

"And don't do anything you'll regret." She laughed, then stopped. "Wait. What am I saying? Go for it. Hang from the chandeliers, order up some whipped cream and kinky toys. You of all people deserve it."

Mariah was still laughing as she hung up. She wasn't into kinky, but a few more nights like last night would be fabulous.

She walked over to the window and looked out over the backyard to the little house where her man of the moment was working out.

When they had been in the suite, it had been all romance all the time. But now they were home. Would things be different? Awkward? After all, he wasn't caring for her anymore—the invalid Mariah, that is. No, now they were lovers, friends, sharing each other.

She pushed away from the window and went to her computer, switched it on. When emotions ran high, she looked to her work for focus and perspective. Sure, she had a love affair going on, but her client was counting on her for help.

She had to win this case. And though the pictures Zayad's friend had taken might not help her win it, perhaps there was something in there that might help or get her thinking.

She snatched up the fax Zayad had tossed on the counter next to her mail, and settled into a chair to study it.

Sweat dripped down Zayad's temple to his jaw as he wielded his sword. Slashing left, then right and right again as he moved across the hardwood floors. His breath coming heavily, he made a quick turn, shot the blade to the ceiling and thrust it back down, halting just centimeters from the curve of a ripe apple.

He grinned. Yes, his son would do well with this sword.

The thought of Redet brought on more thoughts of family, and as Zayad reached for a towel on a side table, he realized that just two days remained until his sister returned. He had found out much from Mariah and was ready to know Jane for himself, ready to tell her the truth and take her back home.

He had not left room for her to refuse him and her title. He could not. Duty remained above all else, and Jane must understand this fact, too.

He held up the Scottish sword, turned his wrist to see its lines.

He recalled something his father had once said. "The heart of every blade is the steel from which it is forged." This blade was a combination of iron and carbon, a perfect blend that allowed him power and flexibility. In the ancient days, power had been most important. But as times changed and people opened their minds to new ideas, a balance was needed. Zayad and his people also had changed to serve the times.

Zayad glanced out the bay window to his right. Afternoon had melded into sunset without his knowledge. It was always thus when he took his exercise.

In that moment, his mind left politics and focused on something far more pleasing. Mariah. He had only two days left with her and he wanted them to be as wonderful and as pleasurable for her as possible. Surely when she found out why he was here and why he had not been forthcoming about his identity, she would want nothing more to do with him.

His gut clenched. He was a fool, but he did not want her to know who he was. He wanted things to remain as they were.

For the first time in his life someone was not aware of his role, his fortune, his title. Mariah cared for him as a man, not as a prince. And for that he would always be in her debt. Starting with her court case.

"Dinnertime."

Zayad turned, and his body went rock hard, fast.

There she stood, moonlight at her back, draped in a thin white cotton tank and little white cotton shorts. She looked ready for bed, not for dinner.

But then again, he mused as he walked to her, he could always be persuaded to eat dessert first.

Twelve

"**I** was wondering where we'd end up," Mariah said, burrowing deeper into the warmth of his chest.

Last night they had forgotten all about dinner and had gone straight to bed, where they'd quickly stripped back the sheets, then stripped each other bare.

Two hours later they'd fallen asleep. Two hours after that Mariah had woken Zayad up with a kiss in a very sweet, very sensitive spot.

Needless to say, the rest of the night had pretty much followed this pattern.

Zayad kissed the top of Mariah's head. "What is this 'end up'?"

She laughed. "Between our two apartments. I wondered if we were going to end up in your bed or in mine."

"Ah, well, as long as we are in bed together, yes?"

"Oh, yes."

Dawn broke with resplendency outside her picture window, and Mariah sighed. She watched the morning's creamy yellow light creep in and hint at a beautiful day. A bright sunny day was always in favor, but for Mariah it really wouldn't matter if a hurricane blew in. She wasn't about to let anything bring her mood down. She was savoring the time she had left. She had just one day with her man until Jane returned and things got different and…well, back to normal. There would be questions asked—questions she didn't even want to look at, much less answer right now.

Since the day she'd smashed into this amazing man, she'd been having the time of her life. And as long as the fantasy kept rolling along in this perfect manner, she had a ticket to ride.

She let her hand trail down Zayad's chest to his belly, let her fingers brush over his navel. "I like sleeping in the same bed with you," she said, having no fear of how vulnerable she sounded. "I thought I'd never like sharing a bed. I've grown accustomed to being alone, sleeping alone, living alone."

"You do not live alone."

"I wasn't talking about sharing space. I meant inside my heart. I'm alone inside my heart. By choice, of course, but…"

"There is comfort in being alone at times. Even in the heart. Sometimes such detachment protects us, no?"

"You bet." She sighed, slid her knee across his thigh, the weight of her boot slowing the process a bit. "I spent four years protecting myself, maybe longer."

"And now?"

"I don't want to do it anymore."

"Even if that means being hurt again?"

"Even if that means getting my heart shredded to bits."

Zayad put a hand to her face and tilted her head, looked at her with complete bewilderment. "How can you say this after all you have been through?"

"Because I've been slowly dying these past four years. Sure, I was protecting myself all the while. But a life built out of fear is no life at all."

"I try not to think such thoughts."

"Why? Because you believe that things shouldn't change or because you're afraid of what will happen if they do?"

He stiffened, and the light, loving mood of a moment ago was lost.

"I'm sorry." She shook her head. "That was wrong and pushy of me. It's your life, your choice."

He gave her a dusty, glum smile. "We do what we must. And our changes come in our own time."

She nodded, then put her head back on his chest. He was right. Even though he had been the impetus to her change, her acceptance of life after a hideous divorce, maybe he wasn't ready to move away from his tricky history. Maybe, like her, he needed to fall in love to get there.

Her heart actually squeezed with pain, but she mentally shook it off. Zayad may not love her, but, unlike her ex and the losers in the courtroom, he had integrity. He'd never promised her anything, never told her he loved her, then snatched away her trust by cheating and lying.

No. He just wasn't ready.

She came up on her elbow, gave him a winning, playful smile. He had done so much for her, been a caretaker, a friend, a lover. If he was going back home in the next week or so, she wanted to make sure he wouldn't forget her—or the time they'd spent together.

"Any plans for today?" she asked.

"Yes."

Oh.

She looked away. Of course he had other things to do. Not every day could be a play day. And she could use the time to work and clean up the house and…

His hand was on her cheek, his thumb brushing over her lower lip. "After my physician takes a look at your beautiful ankle, I have plans with you, mi'nâr."

"Are you going to tell me what that means?"

"Perhaps one day." His sexy black eyes crinkled at the corners as he grinned. "I was thinking about the beach."

Her heart skipped and she smiled in return. "A picnic lunch?"

"Yes, with a little wine perhaps."

"And sand-castle making."

His brow furrowed. "What is this sand castle?"

"You don't know what a—" She waved her hands, tried to look aghast, but just ended up laughing. "I'll show you. You're gonna love it. After all, it's an artistic endeavor."

Zayad sat back in the warm sand and smiled. He was excessively proud of his work, but today that did not seem to be enough.

Curious.

He had never needed anyone's approval.

He glanced at Mariah, magnificent in a pale blue bikini, her curves making him tight with need, her smile making him wonder if true happiness might not be possible after all. She was different from any woman he had ever known. He would admit this much. He also would acknowledge that he wanted her opinion, her praise.

No. He needed it.

Gesturing toward the shape he had created in the sand, he asked, "How does my structure look?"

"Fabulous," she said, her hair whipping in the breeze like a golden sail. "It looks like something out of a Disney movie."

"Does it? Well, this is no imitation of a movie set, mi'nâr. This is the sultan's palace in Emand."

"Really?" She looked impressed.

"Without the wondrous gardens, swimming pools and other exterior additions."

"Of course." She laughed. "Well, it's pretty fancy, not too mention insanely enormous. The sultan must get lost just getting up to brush his teeth."

"I am sure he knows his way." Zayad's gut clenched. This charade had started out with purpose and understanding, but now it had turned into a lie. A cover-up. He was not proud of this. He did not want to continue deceiving Mariah. He cared for her too much now. He would tell her the truth. Tonight.

For a moment he wondered why he had not revealed himself sooner. He knew it was not because Mariah would tell Jane before he had his chance. Well, it might have been initially. But over the past few days he had wanted nothing to interfere with their affair. Nothing. Not even his duty, not even his honor.

The knowledge clawed at him like a Feron scorpion. He had deliberately cast aside the good of his country for this woman, and his principles for their pleasure. Perhaps it was good he was leaving soon.

"Is this a new palace," Mariah asked, tugging him from his thoughts. "Or one of those ancient places you read about in the history books?"

"To the people of Emand, it is timeless. The royal family has lived in the palace for centuries."

"Do you know their history pretty well?"

"I do."

"The current sultan—is he old? Does he have several wives and many kids?"

"Actually he is unmarried. And in Emand, though the old customs are still accepted, the royal family has always taken just one spouse."

She smiled as a wave crashed behind her. "I like that."

"Yes, most Americans do."

She laughed. "And I like you."

His chest went tight at the compliment. A simple compliment. But it held great truth and significance. This woman did not know that the man they spoke of, the wealthy prince who lived in a golden palace, was the very same man who had made love to her all through the night, the same man who wanted more than anything to make love to her again right here, right now.

No.

She thought him an ordinary man and she liked him.

He took her hand and kissed the palm. "What else do you wish to know?"

"Have you seen this sultan up close?"

"I have."

"What's he like? Dictatorial, fierce, demanding?" Her eyes shined with intrigue.

"He has a country to watch over, Mariah. There are times when he must be all of those things."

She nodded. "Of course. It's funny, we make royalty and love so romantic, but it isn't always that."

"It is rarely that…I imagine."

"What an incredibly hard job. But I'm sure he has many advisors to help him."

"Many, but surprisingly they are not as competent as he would like." He knew he should stop at that, but he did not. It was glorious to speak of such matters with a true friend. "This can be a source of frustration for him. Emand has many social-rights issues he wishes to address. It is not easy to turn around centuries of fears and prejudices and foolish ideas. But things are slowly coming along."

She grabbed a bottle of suntan lotion and squeezed a bit out into her hand. "This sounds like one forward-thinking sultan."

Her admiration pleased him. "I am proud to say that he is."

She dabbed the sunscreen on her cheeks and nose. "To right many wrongs, to help closed-minded people see beyond their senseless fears—that's a great job." Suddenly her shoulders fell, and she sighed. "It was the job I set out to do."

"You have." He reached for her and pulled her into his arms. "And you will continue to do this."

"I hope so."

"Enough of these low spirits now." He helped her to her feet, grabbed her hand. "Come with me."

"Where?"

"Do you not like surprises, mi'nâr?"

Mariah warmed at this new and wonderful endearment Zayad kept calling her, and she squeezed his hand. "I never have liked surprises much, but the ones you keep cooking up are slowly changing my mind."

He turned to her and gave a little bow. "I hope that I may always grant you extraordinary surprises."

All thoughts of work and fears of failure were snatched away in the salty breeze. Mariah shivered with excitement as they walked away from the seaside and their castles and into the beach grass.

"I found this place the day after I moved here," Zayad told her as he led her down the side of a small-ish sandy hill.

The sound of the waves crashing against the shore still clung in the air, but no longer were they amongst the public. Zayad had found a private refuge, a lovely cave.

The hollowed-out rock before them beckoned for strangers to enter, and they did. Mariah had no clue what to expect—damp, smelly, dead fish…who knew?

But she couldn't have been more wrong.

All the seaweed and wet earth and rock she'd expected had been cleared away. In the center of the cave, sitting atop clean sand, was a large and very colorful carpet. And on top of the carpet was a picnic lunch.

Actually it was a feast. Meats and cheeses, salad and fruit and cake and wine. She could see this very well indeed, as there were several gashes in the rock wall where seductive little shards of sunlight peeked in.

She'd never seen anything like it and imagined she never would again.

Zayad urged her to sit on the carpet, a shaft of warm sunlight piercing her shoulder and thigh. "I thought we should have our privacy," he said, falling down beside her.

She took in his hard chest and sinewy thighs and fairly sighed with desire. "How did you do this? When did you do this?"

He grinned, took a piece of melon from a plate. "I asked a few…friends to assist me."

"Nice friends. This is incredible."

"I am glad it pleases you." He guided the sweet melon into her mouth.

Didn't he understand that he constantly pleased her? "You've spoiled me for other men, Zayad."

She hadn't meant to say that aloud. She'd been trying to be playful, complimentary—and maybe, in some crazy way, honest about how much she cared for him, how over-the-moon in love with him she was.

But there was nothing playful in those black eyes of his. No, they burned with ire.

"I do not want to think of you with another man," he said gravely.

"Neither do I." Hell, she didn't want to think about another guy for the rest of her life. "Or you with another woman."

"I want no other woman."

"I know. Not now, but—"

He put his hand on hers. "Please. Let us eat, yes? I despise this subject."

So did Mariah, but she couldn't stop herself from going there, from thinking about his future and hers without him in it. But she knew she must. If only to preserve their last day together. "This spread is something else. And I'm starved." She grinned, leaned in and kissed him, hoped that her gesture would inch them toward playful once again. "I've worked up an appetite building that palace."

He tossed her a wry grin. "Did you now?"

"Yep."

He raised an eyebrow.

"Fine, I wasn't actually involved in the building part, but I did haul all that sand and water. You got to give me that."

"Yes, I give you that." He looked as though he wanted to say more, but he didn't. He filled a plate with food and handed it to her. "Come. Let me serve you."

They ate their pretty picnic lunch. They talked about her case, his art and their shared penchant for raspberries. Time flew by and before they knew it, afternoon had appeared, taking away the pretty sunshine and replacing it with shady beams of gray and the drumming sounds of rain on the cave's roof.

Mariah cleared away the dishes and placed them at the entrance to the cave. When she returned to the carpet, she eyed Zayad, looking all too handsome with his black swim trunks, mussed black hair and fiery gaze. "Looks like we're not going anywhere for a while."

The left side of his mouth tipped up. "Are you content with this?"

"Being stuck with you, you mean?"

He nodded.

"I think so." She turned coy and flirtatious and sank to her knees at the edge of the carpet, her fingers playing with the straps of the modest bikini top she'd bought on her way to the beach this morning. "But what shall we do?"

With a full-fledged grin attached, he crawled toward her, an animal stalking its prey. "I can think of several things."

She scooted back playfully. "Like what?"

Quick as a cat, he had his arm about her. He flipped her to her back and rested his chin on her belly. "This."

He kissed her hot skin.

"That's nice," she said, her breath in her throat.

He tugged down her bathing suit bottom, grazed his teeth over her hip bone. "And this."

"Yes." It was more of a squeak than a word, but she didn't care. She loved when he nibbled and suckled and tasted, made her forget everything and just enjoy. Unable to stop herself, she squirmed beneath him, thrust her hips up.

And he answered her call.

His eyes on hers, he eased down her bathing suit. "And this."

"Yes, Zayad. Please." Never in her life had she begged for something, especially something so intimate. Maybe she'd always thought she didn't deserve this kind of love, that she wasn't sexy enough, desirable enough…

Zayad's gaze flickered to the tuft of soft curls between her legs. "Yes, this could keep me occupied for hours."

Mariah could say no more, think no more, as he eased her apart and slid his tongue inside her. Deep and deeper still, until she couldn't breathe. His hands slid under her buttocks and he squeezed.

She sucked in air.

He eased out of her and blew his warm breath over the tense bundle of nerves at her core. "You taste like heaven, mi'nâr."

She moaned, fisted sand.

Slowly, achingly slowly, he slid his tongue upward, between her wet folds. Back and forth so slowly, building her toward the most intense climax of her life.

"Zayad, please," she begged.

"What is it you need?"

"You…faster…please."

"I cannot." He swept his tongue back over her. "I must go slow."

The intensity burned inside her. Her nipples were hard beneath her bathing suit top. Wet heat leaked from her onto the carpet. And outside the cave the waves roared and crashed against the sand while the rain continued to fall.

And then Zayad raised the stakes.

His tongue on her, his breath on her, he took his hand from beneath her bottom and slipped three fingers inside her.

Mariah shook, shuddered, grabbed a fist full of his hair and rode him, bucked against him. Zayad pushed deeper and she couldn't hold on. With a cry she climaxed against his mouth.

In the glowing aftermath, Mariah reached for him, wanted him to slip inside her. But surprisingly and sadly he didn't. Instead he held her tightly against him, kissed her hair and followed her into sleep.

Thirteen

The road was puddle after puddle, and Zayad wished he were back in the cave beside, beneath or on top of Mariah.

But good things had to come to end, yes?

And as the afternoon had worn on and the rain had subsided, they both had known it was time to go. Once in the car, Zayad had secured Mariah in her seat with the seat belt, a blanket and a kiss, then headed away from the beach and toward home.

Now only the sound of the radio could be heard as they drove. He thought about what would happen when they got home, when Jane returned tomorrow. Mariah was doing a little work beside him. She scanned the photographs Zayad's man had taken of her client's cheating ex-husband. She looked contemplative and uneasy. Zayad felt suddenly protective of her and wished she would put the photos away and talk to him. There were issues they had yet to discuss—not amusing issues but important ones. For instance, she had not asked him why he'd pulled her into his arms after making love to her in the cave, instead of pulling her beneath him. He knew it was on her mind. It was certainly on his. If she did ask, he was prepared to say that he had no protection. Which was the truth.

But there was more.

Much more.

He *had* been ready to make love to her, with or without protection. He had wanted to feel her inside and out, with no barriers, and had been ready to damn the consequences.

This fact had scared the life out of him, and he had forced back his desire and given her all the pleasure he could afford.

If he were honest with himself, he would admit that Mariah Kennedy had captured his heart—or what remained of it—and that he did not want to leave California in one week's time.

"Ohmigod!"

The outburst had Zayad jerking to attention. He glanced her way. "What's wrong?"

She was holding up a photograph, staring intently at it. "I can't believe this."

"What is it?" Zayad asked.

"There is something here." She shook the photograph, grinned. "Something we missed before."

"What?"

"Or something I missed."

"Mariah, you make me crazy," Zayad said, exasperation threading his tone. "Suspense in such matters as these is cruel."

"Sorry." She grimaced. "What we've got here is a blue Tiffany's box and an engagement ring."

"I do not understand." Zayad pulled off the main road and shoved the truck into Park.

"Look at this." She pointed to the photograph of the cheating couple at dinner. "He's slipping a ring on her finger."

Zayad took a closer look. It was as she said. The man was placing a small diamond on the woman's left hand. "Yes, I see. But as you said before, this man's proposal happened in the present. He and your client are now divorced. It does not matter if he is with another woman."

Pure childlike excitement glistened in her tiger's eyes. "Unless he bought this for his mistress when he was still married."

Zayad paused, thought about this. "Go on."

"In the credit-card statements I went through during their marriage, there was a charge from Tiffany's. When I asked my client about it, she told me she knew all about it and that it was just a birthday present for herself and the twins—they all have the same birthday. And the amount didn't raise suspicion because he'd always given her and her children extravagant gifts." Mariah shrugged. "So I didn't check it out."

Zayad shook his head. "I do not understand. He obviously did purchase these gifts."

"Yes, but maybe he added a small engagement ring to the bill knowing his wife would never check a birthday gift charge."

Her meaning became clear as glass and Zayad grinned. "You are brilliant."

She blushed. "Nah."

He laughed, momentarily forgetting that he did not belong with this woman, and allowed himself the pleasure of basking in her happiness. "I knew you could do this." His gaze swept over her covetously. "My man is still digging. Perhaps he will find something more on this man's past, and with this new development you have unearthed, your client will have her children yet."

Mariah grunted him the most beautiful of smiles. "Yes, I'm starting to think that could really happen."

"What did I tell you?"

"That I might just win this case."

"And you will listen to me more often, yes?"

She shrugged, said playfully, "Maybe."

"Maybe?" He pulled her into his arms and kissed her breathless as rain began to fall once again against the windshield. "I want you," he uttered.

"I want you, too, but——"

"But perhaps we should get home?"

She moved to his ear and nibbled gently. "Car sex always sounds like fun, but I can't think it actually would be."

He grinned. "Agreed," he said, though at this particular moment, with Mariah's breath and teeth against his ear, he did not care overmuch about where he yanked down his zipper and placed her atop him. But it was her wish that they wait, and until he left, she was his princess. He would do as she bid him. "We should both take a few hours of work, yes? Then find each other for dinner?"

She nodded, her eyes flashing almond fire. "And dessert?"

"Raspberries?"

"Yes." Her gaze moved over his face. At first she looked hungry for more than raspberries, but then a look of melancholy shuttered her eyes.

"What is it?" he asked.

She shook her head. "It's nothing."

"Tell me."

She took in a breath. "I don't know. I've just never known a man so unselfish."

Unselfish? She could not be speaking of him, especially not when it came to her. All his moments, his choices, had been based on what was best for him—for his country, though they were one and the same.

Turning from her, he pulled away from the curb and back onto the road.

"And so supportive," she continued.

His fingers gripped the steering wheel. "I am none of these things."

"You are. The men I've known would never be so supportive."

"Your ex-husband did not support your work?"

"No way."

"Why do you think this was?"

"He never liked competition, in work or out."

Zayad sniffed arrogantly. "He wished to feel all-powerful over you, over his life. This is sad. He was a fool."

"For a long time I thought this was just how men were." She put her hand on his and he shuddered. "But you don't need to feel all-powerful, do you?"

The question nearly forced a brittle laugh from him. He was ruler in his country. He *was* all-powerful. But did he need this from those he cared for, women who were talented and intelligent and could debate and prevail? He believed not. Not now… "Everyone wishes to feel strong and competent in their lives, and I will admit in my younger years I exerted my authority over others for personal gain. But this childishness has thankfully left me."

"I'm glad. It's no way to live." She squeezed his hand, played with his fingers, then asked, "When did it leave you?"

He could have tossed out an answer—ten, twelve, fifteen years of age. But that was not true. The woman who had borne his child had been the one to send him out of childhood and into manhood. This and Redet were his only reasons for wishing the woman well.

As he pulled into their driveway, he said, "At twenty-one I was forced to realize that love and respect could not be commanded, forced or cajoled. It was a good lesson and one I intend to teach my son."

Admiration and something fearfully close to love swam in her magnificent eyes. He wanted to look away, did not want to see how she felt, did not want to get lost in her.

But for a moment he could not help himself.

Thankfully she turned and grabbed the door handle. "I'd better get to work. See if my assumptions are correct."

He nodded. "I had a wonderful day."

"So did I. Thank you."

Without thought he leaned in, kissed her tenderly on the mouth, then let her go.

It was only after she had closed the front door of her side of the duplex that the irony of that gentle action hit him full force.

Later that night they dined at her small but cute kitchen table. It was no cave with carpets and ocean strains, but Mariah had made the setting as romantic as she could. Candles and flowers from the backyard, wine goblets and Tara's silver.

She was pretty sure she'd done a bang-up job until Zayad said, "You are the very worst cook, Mariah Kennedy. A wonderful legal brain with legs to make a man sweat, but a cook—sadly no."

Mariah laughed. "I know. I'm completely hopeless. You didn't think it was possible to screw up spaghetti, did you?"

He held up a piece of limp pasta with his fork. "How long was this pasta cooking?"

"I got distracted."

"With work?"

No, not work, she thought. With him. Her brain was all about him. But she couldn't tell him that. She couldn't tell him that she'd been sitting at the kitchen table contemplating the future—specifically the weeks after Zayad left. No, she'd already billed herself as head over heels for him. Her eyes fairly dripped with love. She sure didn't need to tell him about her future career as a salesgirl for the self-help tapes *Pining for the Perfect Man.*

She filled his wineglass, then gave him another piece of bread. "Yes, I was thinking about my case."

"Do not worry, Mariah. I have told you it will go

smoothly. Especially now that you have spotted the flaw."

"You're right. I know you're right."

"It is a rare occurrence, but it does happen." He grinned. "You have confirmed the Tiffany's receipt, yes?"

"Yep. It was just as I'd thought."

"Very good."

A sudden breeze shot in through the open kitchen windows, sending the candle flames into a wild dance. Here they were having dinner again, kind of like normal people. A couple. Yet they were anything but normal and they certainly weren't a couple.

Mariah's heart dipped and she decided to switch topics. "So, have you spoken to your son?"

"Just one hour ago, as a matter of fact."

"How is he?"

"He is well. But I will see for myself soon enough."

She nodded, swallowed hard. Maybe they needed to get this out in the open, say what was on both of their minds.

Obviously Zayad thought so, too. He reached across the table, took her hand. "I miss my son and my home, yet…"

"Yes?" she said, foolishly hopeful.

"The thought of leaving fills me with a deep sadness."

"So don't leave," she said with a light chuckle, though she felt anything but light.

"I must." He took a swallow of wine. "It is complicated, Mariah."

"It always is." She eased her hand from his and

started gathering up the plates still heavy with her droopy pasta.

He grabbed her wrist. "Do not revert back inside yourself."

"I'm not."

"You are. For days you have been free and easy and happy."

Didn't he get it? Free, easy, happy, sexy, desired— it all came with him.

"I want you to understand my position," he said, clearly unwilling to release her so she could pout and pretend his departure meant nothing.

"I do understand, Zayad. You have Redet and a life there—"

"I *must* be in Emand. You are right—my life is there." A struggle went on behind his eyes. "A responsibility that is unlike any other. Now, if you wished to come with me, that would be a different—" He stopped cold, his dark skin going ashen. "What I mean to say—"

"No, please." She stopped him right there. She couldn't hear him take that back. Not if she didn't want to cry herself to sleep for the next two months. "Let's not say anything more tonight, okay? I can't hear you backtrack and I can't hear myself help you do it."

"Mariah…"

"Please. Let's just enjoy tonight."

He nodded, then gently coaxed her from her dishes onto his lap and into his arms.

By the flickering light of a single bedside candle Zayad pushed into Mariah's body. Hot, tight and wet, she closed around him, embraced his erection.

He groaned, a deep muffled sound against her neck.

He took her mouth, made love to her lips, her tongue, as he raised his hips, then thrust into her again.

His body was weak tonight and he couldn't wait. As soon as he felt her shudder beneath him, he quickened his thrusts and let his head drop back. His body shook, the sweet headiness of orgasm taking him while he allowed his mind to fall wonderfully blank.

Fourteen

"**H**oney, I'm home."

A woman's cheerful voice rang through the duplex like a thousand bells. Zayad stirred beneath the sheets, trying to register the sound and where it had come from, but his mind was still muffled from the lack of sleep last night, as he had paid sweet penance for his slip in control the first time around.

Rolling to his side, he reached out for Mariah but snagged only cool sheets. On alert now, he looked up, bright sunlight accosting his vision. She was gone and he was alone. His chest felt heavy. For the first time in his life he did not like waking up alone. It was a dangerous admission, but sleeping beside Mariah had been wonderful, and he would not mind if such an occurrence happened every night.

He shuffled out of bed and reached for his clothes. He threw on his pants and yawned. He was still buttoning his shirt as he walked into the living room.

But it was not the woman he expected to see lounging on the couch, leafing through a pile of mail. It was a woman he had longed to see, a woman who shared Sakir's long, lean body and his youngest brother's full mouth.

The beautiful dark-haired young woman looked up, startled. "Oh, hello."

"Hello." Such intensity of feeling ran through his blood as he looked at her. "You must be Jane."

"Yep, but you're not Mariah."

Humor glistened in her eyes. In that, she was her mother's daughter. His heart squeezed. His baby sister stood before him, and he was practically speechless.

She inspected him. "So, you're the man who's making my roommate's heart go pittypat."

"Pittypat?" Confusion hit him and he shook his head. "I surely do not pity her?"

She laughed. "No, no. It's an expression of how a heart beats. I meant Mariah likes you, that's all."

"Ah. Sometimes the English slang is unintelligible."

"For me, too, sometimes." She glanced around. "So, where is Mariah?"

"I am not entirely sure, but if I had to guess, I would say she went to check on something for her case."

Jane sighed. "Always working. I hope the two of you did more than work while I was gone."

He sat in the chair opposite her. "There was much time spent on folly."

Her grin widened and she grabbed a picture of her

and Mariah off the side table. "Good. She needs folly, and by the look of it—" she glanced up "—so do you."

He returned her grin. She had humor and fire in her blood. She had the soul of an Al-Nayhal—wise, quick. His father would be proud. "Perhaps we can discuss something else? I do not wish to speak of my time with Mariah." The thought of leaving her was killing him, and the sooner he dealt with the reason for his coming in the first place, the better.

Jane shrugged. "Okay." Though in her eyes he saw a little unease.

"Let us talk of you." He sat forward in his chair, ready to hear the wishes and dreams straight from his sister's lips. "Tell me of your passions and your pursuits. How long have you been a chef?"

She looked uncomfortable now but did not evade the question. "Five years."

"I am sure you are very good at it."

"I don't know."

"I know," Zayad said with deep conviction. The Al-Nayhal family excelled at their pursuits. "And you wish to open a restaurant, I hear?"

"Yes, I do." She looked around, at the door, at the picture of her and her friend. "Who told you that? Mariah?"

"Mariah and your mother."

Her head popped back. "You met my mother?"

"On two occasions. She is wonderful."

"She is. The best parent a girl could have."

"As was your father—"

She shook her head almost vehemently. "I never knew the man. He died before I was born."

Zayad crossed his arms over his chest. "Is that so?"

* * *

Mariah stood at the open window and listened, her heart fading back into its protective, sullen and miserable shell.

"I do not wish to speak of my time with Mariah. Let us talk of you."

And said with such caring, such deep curiosity, no one could deny he was interested.

Mariah sagged against the faded white stucco and fought teary as she listened to him prattle on about what a great chef Jane had to be. Mariah didn't understand. She didn't get how this amazing man who had cared for her, spoiled her, made love to her, was now royally hitting on her roommate.

And yet she could understand.

Her life had been full of these guys, just no one as smooth as this one. And she'd actually thought herself in love with him. How could she have fallen for another player? A guy so obviously into conquest—*get this one all hot, bothered and head over heels, then drop her. The chase is over. Move on to the next one.*

Her heart thudded in her chest, and she wanted to run away. She hated this feeling, this jumpy sensation, that life was about to come crashing down into a jagged pile of reality.

But even though the instinct to bolt was strong, she'd changed. She wasn't the fearful, angry, bitchy lawyer anymore. She'd felt love again and liked it, regardless of the pain it was bringing on now. There was no way she could run away this time.

Her hand shook a bit as she opened the front door,

her smile, too, as she saw her roommate—who looked beyond uncomfortable and a just a bit pissed off.

"Welcome back, Jane."

A smile creased Jane's face, and she stood up, ran over to Mariah and gave her a hug. "Oh, M, it's good to see you."

"You, too." Mariah pulled back from her. "Listen, can I have a minute with Zayad?"

Complete understanding and support glittered in Jane's eyes and she nodded. "Sure, I'll go unpack. Pizza and a movie later?"

"You're on."

Jane didn't even wave at Zayad. She was up the stairs in an instant, her door closed.

When Mariah found Zayad's gaze, she wasn't surprised to see him grinning at her. Still as charming as ever. Heck, he even had the balls to look as if he had missed her.

He motioned for her to come to him. "You were out of bed early."

But she remained where she was. "I wanted to hit the library."

"Did you find what you were looking for?"

"I did." She took a deep breath. "I also found what I was looking for here at home."

Confusion stripped his features. "I am sorry."

"Yes, you are." Nervously, she crossed her arms over her chest, then released them to her sides. No barriers, no protection. Not this time. "Look, Zayad, I was listening outside the window. I heard you with Jane. I heard your compliments and I heard your come-ons." She laughed, but there was little humor there. "Jeez, I'm such an idiot. I suspected you wanted Jane from the beginning—I mean, who wouldn't with all those questions. But then when you showed interest in me, I thought maybe I'd imagined your interest in Jane. But obviously I was wrong. You were just making time with me until she was back, right? Until another woman came along, right?"

His black eyes went serious and he stood up, walked over to her. "What you are suggesting is impossible."

Oh, the arrogance, "I just heard you, Zayad, 'Let's not speak of Mariah. Let's talk about you, your passions.' Blah blah blah. That's pretty clear."

"It may seem that way, however this whole thing is anything but clear."

"Don't play word games with me."

"What you heard was only my concern."

"Concern? For what? You've just met her. You don't know her."

His gaze didn't flicker. He said, "This seems odd, I know. But if you will just trust me—"

"Trust you? C'mon, Zayad. You know me. You know what I've been through with my lying, cheating ex-husband. After what I just heard, you think trusting you is actually a practical request?"

The doorbell rang.

Then again.

Mariah didn't move.

Zayad raised a brow. "Shall I get that?"

"No. I'll go." She shook her head with frustration and embarrassment and plain old grief, then turned and went to the door. "I think we're pretty much done here."

Another coward, Mariah thought as she swung the

door wide. But her thoughts stopped there. Like a scene from a movie, what felt like a hundred flashbulbs erupted in her face.

Fifteen

"**T**hey have found me. Come at once."

Zayad pressed the off button on his cell phone. It was a disaster. First he had made the mistake of turning off the security cameras and commanding his men to back off, as he had wanted more privacy with Mariah. Second he had waited too long to tell Mariah and Jane the truth.

Now he had paparazzi at his door, a sister who thought he was after her and the woman he wanted above all else thinking him a devious rogue.

Though on that last account, she would not be far from the truth.

Jane came running downstairs.

Mariah looked completely incensed. "What the hell is going on here? The press 'found' you?" Total bewilderment etched her features. She gestured toward Jane. "One moment I was accusing you of hitting on—"

"My sister," Zayad said quickly.

"—Jane, and the next there's a bunch of report—" Mariah stopped cold. Her eyebrows smashed together. She swallowed hard, licked her lips. And she just stared at him. "What?"

Coming to stand beside Mariah, Jane fairly choked out, "What?"

A knock on the back door made the women jump. Zayad shook his head. "It is one of my men. If you will excuse me for one moment."

The women said nothing.

Zayad brought Fandal into the room. "This is my chief of security."

"Your chief of security?" Mariah fairly yelled. Then her voice went low and dangerous. "I'm only going to ask you this once more and then I'm letting all those reporters out there inside to have at you. What the hell is going on!"

He had not wanted it this way, but he had little choice. "My name is Zayad Al-Nayhal. I am the sultan of Emand."

He watched the blood drain from Mariah's face. Jane looked completely confused.

"Several weeks ago," he explained, "my father's aide made a deathbed confession." He wished he could hold Mariah close as he spoke, but she looked as though she had cactus thorns growing out of her. "He claimed my father, on a trip to California, met an American woman and spent three days in her company. He also claimed the woman became pregnant and unbeknownst to my father gave birth to a child."

Mariah shook her head. "I don't understand."

"I already knew who she was when I left Emand. But before I told her the truth, I wanted to know her, see who she was and what she stood for." He looked over at Jane, who seemed ready to collapse. "I wanted to see if she would take her rightful place beside her brothers."

Jane fairly whimpered. She shook her head over and over. "No, I'm not… It's not possible."

"It is fact, my sister," Zayad said.

"My father died—"

"He did pass on, but far after you were born."

"My mother would've told me this. She wouldn't have lied to me."

Zayad remembered Tara's face when she had explained her reasoning, her fears. "She protected you. The aide never told my father of you and he lied to Tara. He told her that my father wanted nothing to do with the baby or the mother. So, you see, your mother was acting under the assumption that your father had denounced you. She only lied to protect your heart."

Jane looked stricken and stunned. "And why did *you* lie, Zayad?"

"I thought it best not to disclose my identity. I felt it was important to see who you were before—"

"To see if I was worthy, right?"

His chin lifted. "Yes."

They continued to talk, argue, question and answer, but Mariah couldn't listen anymore. She was thoroughly confused and very hurt. She slipped from the room, went through the kitchen and into the backyard. The large security man saw her but didn't try to stop her. She pushed past him and ran. She didn't know how she got very far considering she couldn't breathe all that well. But she kept running until she reached the back house. Once there, she went inside, saw Zayad's swords—shiny, beautiful, impenetrable—and collapsed on the wood floor, head in hands.

It was all a lie. Sure, he hadn't wanted to date Jane, but he'd wanted her all the same and he'd used Mariah to get her. She remembered all the questions, the interest in Tara. He hadn't cared about Mariah's foot. He'd wanted to find out about Jane, get easy access to her from her mother and best friend.

Tears pricked her eyes and she felt sick to her stomach. She'd done it again. Allowed another wealthy, charming, irresistible man to win her over and screw her up.

What a loser she was.

The door to the house opened and light spilled into the room.

"I know what you must be thinking."

She sniffed. "Get out."

"I will be as honest as I can."

"Well, that'll be a first."

He sat down beside her on the floor.

"Should princes really be sitting on the floor?" she asked, ire in her tone.

"Please curb your hostility for one moment."

She glared at him.

He sighed. "Yes, it started out as a ruse to gain information about Jane. But you must believe that everything changed that day in Ojai. I felt strong feelings for you, and they have only gained in strength."

She hated the lift in her heart and quashed it instantly. "Yet you continued to lie to me."

"I did. I felt I could not reveal who I was and who Jane was until she returned."

"You told Tara, didn't you?"

"She guessed."

"I think this is all a load of garbage."

He touched her hand. "I know you are angry—"

"Angry?" She swatted him away. "I'm beyond angry. You knew what I went through with my ex husband. You knew what I continue to go through with my work and yet you still kept lying."

"Mariah, I am sorry. I so desperately wanted to see my sister, regain my family, I did not think. No, that is not true. Actually I could not stop thinking about my dishonesty to you."

"And yet you continued."

He didn't say anything for a moment. His eyes went somber, his mouth drew into a thin line. "You are right. I was selfish. I did not want our time to end and knew if I told you the truth, you would walk away from me."

"Just like you would've done in one more week anyway."

He looked ashamed. She'd never seen that on a man. And on this man, who was far too proud for his own good, it was a little disturbing.

"Mariah, please." He took her hand. "Believe that I will never lie to you again."

"No, you won't, because I won't give you the chance."

"Mariah, I care for you deeply. I want you to come with me to Emand. I want you to be my wife."

She stilled, her heart smacking against her ribs. He wanted her to be his wife. Oh, how she wanted to fling herself at him and say yes, yes, yes. But there was one hitch. He'd said he cared for her. Was that the same as love? Her belly clenched with pain. Did it even matter at this point?

"Remember what we spoke of that day at the beach?" he said, inching closer to her. "How the sultan needs advisors who believe in the good and who will fight for the basic human rights of others."

"Yes," she uttered, her brain a complete mess.

"We could do so much together."

She stared at him. He was serious. His eyes swam with tenderness. He really did want her, want to marry her. If she forgave him, believed him, she could be this man's wife, love him, have Jane as her true sister. Lord, it all sounded wonderful. It sounded magical. But for a woman with her history, it sounded too good to be true.

"I can't." Tears spilled from her eyes as she eased her hand from his. The fear was too great. She loved this man too much to allow him to hurt her again. "I can't put myself in that position again. It hurts too much."

"You cannot forgive, mi'nâr? Knowing the circumstances?"

She shook her head.

It took him a moment, his jaw tight, but finally he nodded. "I understand. What I did was unforgivable." He laid a file folder down by her feet, then stood. "Fandal just gave these to me. I have not looked at them. I hope you find what you are looking for here."

Mariah stared at the folder. She didn't need to look

inside. She knew there was more than enough information to help her client gain custody of her children. "Thank you."

He nodded, turned to leave, then stopped. "Can you tell me you have no love for me, Mariah?"

Her heart dipped, her throat felt tight and dry. Everything inside her wanted him, wanted to forgive him, wanted to go with him to his beautiful country and have a real family of her own. Everything but her pride. "I'm sorry." She said the words as much to herself as to him.

He didn't turn back. "I cannot stay here any longer. I must leave tonight."

"I understand. Have a safe trip."

"I love you, Mariah Kennedy," were the last words she heard him say before the door to the back house closed and she was alone again with her pride intact but her heart bleeding.

Sixteen

The lights of Emand flickered on before his eyes.

He had hoped to feel a great sense of peace upon returning home, but instead he felt empty.

Mariah had refused him—rightly so after what he had done, but it was a bitter pill to swallow. And then there was Jane. His sister had said she wanted some time to think, to speak with her mother, then to think some more. There was a time when Zayad would have fought that, perhaps coaxed her into coming back with him. But he had not the will to fight her.

Either of them, in fact.

The city lights dimmed before him, and in the thick plastic of his window he saw Mariah's eyes. The image grabbed his gut and twisted. Her eyes were filled with betrayal and confusion and a hope that had gone so hopelessly astray. Zayad turned away from the window. He could not blame Mariah's rejection on anything but his own bad deeds, and for that he hoped he suffered long and hard.

A servant crept in and cleared his untouched dinner tray, then placed a small dish of raspberries and cream in front of him. "Your dessert, Your Royal Highness."

He stared at the red-and-white perfection and wanted to smash it with his fist. He had lost the best thing that had ever happened to him—a friend, a lover, a true companion for life. All in the name of fear.

If he had the power to turn this plane around right now, he would. But he knew that would be no smart move. She needed time to cool, a few weeks perhaps.

Weeks... Pure torture for a man who had fought love for so long, then found the right woman, the one person who filled him completely. His brother, Sakir, had seen Zayad's feelings for Mariah immediately on his short visit to Texas this morning and had tried to coax his brother into talking. But Zayad could only manage the bones of the matter and had left early.

His jaw went rigid, and he pushed the fruit aside. He would not lose her. When he went back for Jane, he would try again.

And again and again. Until Mariah forgave him, accepted him and let herself love him again.

"What's the verdict, Counselor?" Jane asked, simultaneously banging on the bathroom door.

In the two weeks since Zayad had gone, Mariah had experienced pure rage, total despair, unholy loneliness and deep regret, but never had she felt sublime happiness.

Until this moment.

Sitting on the edge of the bathtub, her heart pounding and her hands shaking, she held up the pregnancy test again and spied the results. Nothing had changed. Still two blue lines.

Still pregnant.

"Dammit, M. Let me in."

Mariah rose, felt the water in her legs as she wobbled to the door and opened it.

"So?" Jane said, her eyes bright with excitement.

"You're an auntie."

Jane squealed and hugged Mariah, then squealed again. "I can't believe it."

"I can't, either. We were so careful."

"Things can happen. Providence can take a hand when mere mortals are being stubborn."

Mariah prepared herself for another fight with Jane over her refusal of Zayad, then thought better of it and sat back down on the bathroom floor. "I'm not giving in."

"Fine."

"Seriously."

"Fine."

Mariah sighed. "The bottom line is, he lied to me."

"There is no bottom line in life."

"No fortune-cookie quotes right now, okay?" Mariah said on a heavy chuckle.

Jane sat on the toilet lid. "Okay, so yes. Yes, he lied to you. He made a mistake. But it isn't the end of the world." When Mariah opened her mouth, Jane waved a hand. "He didn't cheat on you, M. He didn't take your dignity and your pride. He's not Alan."

"I know he's not Alan."

"No, I don't think you do."

Mariah looked heavenward, sighed. "Okay. You're right. Maybe I am having a hard time separating them."

Reaching down, Jane put her hand on Mariah's belly. "You've got to now."

A shiver coursed through Mariah. Sitting here in the bathroom, pregnancy test in hand, it felt like one of those defining moments. One where you look back in ten years and say, "Damn, I made a mistake." or "It was the best decision of my life."

She fiddled with the edge of the bath mat. She knew she had some soul-searching to do and some forgiveness to find within her hardened heart. She owed it to herself and to her baby to get past a mistake. "By the way, Auntie Jane, you sound like you've already accepted this whole Al-Nayhal birthright-princess thing."

Jane shrugged. "It's my mother. She's very supportive. I think Zayad made a killer impression on her."

Get in line.

"Anyway," Jane continued, "she told me everything, explained everything, made me see that I am who I am and there's no point in trying to deny it."

"But a whole new family…" Mariah began warily.

"I know." Jane's eyes shined. "Isn't it wonderful? I spoke with Sakir yesterday afternoon. He's amazing and so is his wife."

After studying her friend for a moment, Mariah pointed a finger. "You're going to Emand, aren't you?"

Jane nodded.

"When?"

"Tara and I leave on Friday."

Mariah wilted. "Tara?"

"She wants to see Emand, too. Well, she wants to see it in her way. And it's about time, don't you think?"

Mariah's stomach clenched. Life as she knew it was ending. "And Zayad is okay with Tara coming—"

"It was his idea."

"You talked to him?" Her misery was like a steel weight.

"Last night."

"Did he say anything…?" Mariah shook her head. She wasn't about to ask if he missed her, still loved her, wanted her to come to Emand, too.

But Jane offered the information anyway. "He loves you so much, Mariah."

Mariah shook her head, as if that gesture would erase her friend's words.

Jane persisted, "But he doesn't want to push you."

"Maybe I need the push." Leaning back against the cool tub, Mariah sighed. "What am I going to do, Jane?"

"I can only speak from my own experience."

"Okay, have at it."

Tears welled in Jane's eyes as she knelt beside Mariah, took her hand. "Every child deserves to know their father."

Mariah's jaw dropped and stayed that way as Fandal drove her through the iron gates and up to the sultan's palace. It was just as Zayad had described. Golden towers, a spectacular garden, miles of tawny sand in the distance.

A fairy-tale palace worthy of a magic carpet, a bois-terous genie and, of course, Aladdin.

But this was no fairy tale she was walking into with her heart in her throat. This was real life, and she was about to see for herself what kind of ending it would bring.

After thinking long and hard about her future and the future of her child, she knew there was no other home, no other life she wanted to share than Zayad's. If he'd still have her.

She'd decided to come before Jane and Tara, before their own family began. It was best to be rejected without too many witnesses, she thought, her nerves a wreck as Fandal guided her through several entrancing rooms in the palace.

Finally he held a door open and ushered her inside. "This way, madam."

"Thank you, Fandal," she said, her eyes widening as she stepped into the most beautiful of libraries.

The servant motioned for her to take a seat on a leather couch, and she did. Her gaze moved about the beautiful room, then stopped on a certain piece of art-work. She swallowed, her throat tight.

"Is that an original Hockney?" she asked Fandal.

"Yes, Miss Kennedy. The sultan purchased it when he returned from America. He looks at it often."

"Does he?"

He grinned, nodded. "I am glad you have come," he said. "It will make the sultan feel better."

Her chest went tight with concern. "Feel better? Is he ill?"

Shaking his head, Fandal said, "I should not speak

of it, but I have never seen him so… He works with his swords far too much. And he has lost weight."

She didn't want to hear any more, think any more. She just wanted Zayad. "Fandal, please go and get him."

The man smiled, bowed and left. Mariah leaned back on the couch feeling as though she couldn't breathe. She'd imagined this moment for the entire flight, but for the life of her she hadn't had a clue how it would end.

She heard footsteps in the hall, then Zayad saying, "I told you I did not want to be disturbed, emergency or no. What could possibly be so important—"

She sat up, turned just in time to see him enter the library. She held her breath, waited for a sign of either his love or rejection.

He stared at her. "Mariah?"

She stood up. "I had to come. I had to tell you something."

"What is it?" He looked as pensive as she felt.

She gave him a half smile. "Well, first of all, I won my case. Because of your help, a devoted mother now has her children."

It took him a moment, then a soft smile tugged at his mouth and he walked over to her. "I am glad for this."

With a grin of his own, Fandal left discreetly, shutting the door behind himself.

Zayad was before her, his gaze eating up her face, his eyes dark with unanswered questions and unfulfilled passion. "How did you get here?"

"I spoke with Fandal. He was wonderful. He arranged for me to come."

"He is a good man and will be promoted this very day for what he has done."

Mariah smiled, hope seeping into her pores with every word he uttered. "There's something else. Another reason for my being here."

He reached out, brushed his thumb over her cheek. "Tell me."

"I've brought the sword you left behind."

His gaze was pinned to hers. "Thank you."

"Fandal has it. I thought it was important. You bought it for your son, right?"

"I did."

Confidence sparked her and she took his hands, put them around her waist. "Would you find another, Zayad?"

He sighed, pulled her into his arms and hugged her tightly. "I would buy you anything you wish."

Her pulse jumped. "The sword wouldn't be for me."

"No?"

"No." She took a deep breath, eased herself away from him. Her gaze found his and she found her bold soul. "Do you love me, Zayad?"

His eyes filled with desperation. "More than my life."

Tears filled her eyes and she took his hand, placed it on her belly. "The sword is for our child."

His mouth dropped, his eyes widened. "What?"

"I'm pregnant."

She stared at him, then finally saw what she was so desperate to see, what she had felt for days. Pure joy.

Again he pulled her into his arms, rocked her back and forth, uttered words she didn't understand but could feel in her bones—prayer, thankfulness. "My love, mi'nâr."

"Please tell me what that means, Zayad."

"It means my sweet, my beauty."

She smiled and felt as light as air, felt happy and so in love.

"This is the way it should be," he said. "We are together, you and me and our child."

For several moments they just clung to each other. But Mariah knew there was so much more she needed to say before they could embrace a future together.

She pulled back, touched his face. "I want you to know that I understand why you did what you did."

"Mariah…" He looked so pained, so full of shame.

"I love you, Zayad. I want my child to know both of its parents. I want it to see us as we are now, in love, happy, devoted, able to forgive each other."

"Yes."

"A lifetime of love."

He cupped her face in his hands. "Can you trust me again?"

"Yes, my love. You made a mistake, and I got scared. But someday—probably soon—I'll screw up, too. And you know what?"

"What?" He ran his thumb over her lower lip.

"You'll forgive me, and we'll go on and we'll be a family and we'll love each other through it all."

He kissed her with passion and thanksgiving. "I love you so dearly, Mariah."

"And I love you."

"Marry me?"

"Yes."

"And you will be happy here?"

"I will be happy where you are and our child and Redet. Like you said, there's much work for me to do here, and I'm ready."

"Redet. He is anxious to meet you."

"And I him," she said with real warmth.

"Shall we go and tell my son of our plans, then?"

"Redet is here?" Mariah asked, thoroughly excited to meet the boy.

In Zayad's eyes Mariah saw a man who loved his child deeply and a man who wondered what the future would hold for her and Redet. "My son has always wanted a mother," he said tentatively.

She grinned, her heart so full, so happy. "Well, he's got one. I've always wanted a big family."

Tears pricked his eyes, but for this man of power, tears were not customary. He inhaled deeply. "I love you, dear one. I am the luckiest man in the world."

"I believe we both got lucky."

He kissed her. "Yes."

"I think someone knew that after what we've both been through, maybe we deserved a break. Maybe we deserved some real happiness."

"I do not know if I will ever deserve you." He kissed her again, tenderly this time, then took her hand. "But I will spend a lifetime trying."

Smiles on their faces, hands clasped tightly, they left the library. And with a pleased Fandal at their heels, Zayad led the woman he loved upstairs, into her new home, into a loving family and a wonderful, brave new life.

* * * * *

Silhouette® Desire®

presents

the final installment of

*The Reilly triplets bet they could go
ninety days without sex. Hmm.*

THE LAST
REILLY STANDING

by Maureen Child

(SD #1664, available July 2005)

Aidan Reilly was determined to win the bet
he'd made with his brothers. Three months
without sex meant one thing: spend *a lot* of
time with his best gal pal Terry Evans. She had
given up on love long ago because the pain
just wasn't worth it. Then…temptation proved
to be too much. The last Reilly standing had
lost the bet, but could he win the girl?

Available at your favorite retail outlet.

If you enjoyed what you just read,
then we've got an offer you can't resist!

Take 2 bestselling
love stories FREE!
Plus get a FREE surprise gift!

Clip this page and mail it to Silhouette Reader Service™

IN U.S.A.	IN CANADA
3010 Walden Ave.	P.O. Box 609
P.O. Box 1867	Fort Erie, Ontario
Buffalo, N.Y. 14240-1867	L2A 5X3

YES! Please send me 2 free Silhouette Desire® novels and my free surprise gift. After receiving them, if I don't wish to receive anymore, I can return the shipping statement marked cancel. If I don't cancel, I will receive 6 brand-new novels every month, before they're available in stores! In the U.S.A., bill me at the bargain price of $3.80 plus 25¢ shipping and handling per book and applicable sales tax, if any*. In Canada, bill me at the bargain price of $4.47 plus 25¢ shipping and handling per book and applicable taxes**. That's the complete price and a savings of at least 10% off the cover prices—what a great deal! I understand that accepting the 2 free books and gift places me under no obligation ever to buy any books. I can always return a shipment and cancel at any time. Even if I never buy another book from Silhouette, the 2 free books and gift are mine to keep forever.

225 SDN DZ9F
326 SDN DZ9G

Name	(PLEASE PRINT)	
Address	Apt.#	
City	State/Prov.	Zip/Postal Code

Not valid to current Silhouette Desire® subscribers.

Want to try two free books from another series?
Call 1-800-873-8635 or visit www.morefreebooks.com.

* Terms and prices subject to change without notice. Sales tax applicable in N.Y.
** Canadian residents will be charged applicable provincial taxes and GST.
All orders subject to approval. Offer limited to one per household.
® are registered trademarks owned and used by the trademark owner and or its licensee.

DES04R   ©2004 Harlequin Enterprises Limited

Blaze™

HARLEQUIN® *Blaze*™

Where were you when the lights went out?

Shane Walker was seducing his best friend in:

#194 NIGHT MOVES

by **Julie Kenner** July 2005

Adam and Mallory were rekindling
the flames of first love in:

#200 WHY NOT TONIGHT?

by **Jacquie D'Alessandro** August 2005

Simon Thackery was professing his love...
to his best friend's fiancée in:

#206 DARING IN THE DARK

by **Jennifer LaBrecque** September 2005

24 Hours:
BLACKOUT

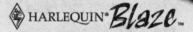

**Welcome to Silhouette Desire's
brand-new installment of**

*The drama unfolds for six of
the state's wealthiest bachelors.*

BLACK-TIE SEDUCTION
by Cindy Gerard
(Silhouette Desire #1665, July 2005)

LESS-THAN-INNOCENT
INVITATION
by Shirley Rogers
(Silhouette Desire #1671, August 2005)

STRICTLY CONFIDENTIAL
ATTRACTION
by Brenda Jackson
(Silhouette Desire #1677, September 2005)

*Look for three more titles from Michelle Celmer,
Sara Orwig and Kristi Gold to follow.*

COMING NEXT MONTH

#1663 BETRAYED BIRTHRIGHT—Sheri WhiteFeather
Dynasties: The Ashtons
When Walker Ashton decided to search for his past, he found it on a
Sioux Nation reservation. Helping him to deal with his Native American
heritage was Tamra Winter Hawk, a woman who cherished her roots
and had Walker longing for a future together. But when his real-world
commitments intruded upon their fantasy liaison, would they find a way
to keep up the connection they'd formed?

#1664 THE LAST REILLY STANDING—Maureen Child
Three-Way Wager
Aidan Reilly was determined to win the bet he'd made with his brothers.
Three months without sex meant one thing: spend *a lot* of time with his
best gal pal, Terry Evans. She had given up on love long ago because the
pain just wasn't worth it. Then…temptation proved to be too much. The last
Reilly standing had lost the bet, but could he win the girl?

#1665 BLACK-TIE SEDUCTION—Cindy Gerard
Texas Cattleman's Club: The Secret Diary
Millionaire Jacob Thorne got on Christine Travers's last nerve—the sensible
lady had no time for Jacob's flirtatious demeanor. But when the two butted
heads at an auction, Jacob embarked on a black-tie seduction that would
prove she had needs—womanly needs—that only he could satisfy.

#1666 THE RUGGED LONER—Bronwyn Jameson
Princes of the Outback
Australian widower Tomas Carlisle was stunned to learn he had to father
a child to inherit a cattle empire. Making a deal with longtime friend
Angelina Mori seemed the perfect solution—until their passion escalated
and Angelina mounted an all-out attack on Tomas's defense against hot,
passionate, *committed* love.

#1667 CRAVING BEAUTY—Nalini Singh
They'd married within mere days of meeting. Successful tycoon
Marc Bordeaux had been enchanted by Hira Dazirah's desert beauty. But
Hira feared Marc only craved her outer good looks. This forced Marc to
prove his true feelings to his virgin bride—and tender actions spoke louder
than words.…

#1668 LIKE LIGHTNING—Charlene Sands
Although veterinarian Maddie Brooks convinced rancher Trey Walker to
allow her to live and work on his ranch, there was no way Trey would ever
romance the sweet and sexy Maddie. He was a victim of the "Walker Curse"
and couldn't commit to any woman. But once they gave in to temptation,
Maddie was determined to make their arrangement more permanent.…

SDCNM0605